Charge It To The Game 3

RIGHT IDEA, WRONG B*TCH

NAI

U.A.D PRESENTS

Stay Up to Date

To stay up to date on new releases, plus get information on contests, sneak peeks and more,

Click the link below...
https://mailchi.mp/6d21003686d1/subscribe

Soundtracks

Scan the QR Code below to listen to the Soundtracks/Singles of some of your favorite U.A.D titles:

Don't have Spotify or Apple Music?
No Sweat!
Visit your choice streaming platform and search URBAN AINT
DEAD.

Currently on lock serving a bid?
JPay, iHeartRadio, WHATEVER!
We got you covered.
Simply log into your facility's kiosk or tablet, go to music and search
URBAN AINT DEAD.

Submission Guidelines

Submit the first three chapters of your completed manuscript to urbanaintdead@gmail.com, subject line: Your book's title. The manuscript must be in a .doc file and sent as an attachment. The document should be in Times New Roman, double-spaced, and in size 12 font. Also, provide your synopsis and full contact information. If sending multiple submissions, they must each be in a separate email. Have a story but no way to submit it electronically? You can still submit to URBAN AINT DEAD. Send in the first three chapters, written or typed, of your completed manuscript to:

URBAN AINT DEAD
P.O Box 448
Maybrook, NY 12543

DO NOT send original manuscript. Must be a duplicate.
Provide your synopsis and a cover letter containing your full contact information.
Thanks for considering URBAN AINT DEAD.

Chapter One

MAHOGANY

Hearing my father's voice on the other end of the phone was a shock in itself but hearing that my baby had been snatched up stunned me into silence. I couldn't respond verbally. Instead, I ended the call, completely disregarding Mo on the other line. Nothing else mattered in this present moment. The fact that someone was bold enough to snatch my fucking kid up let me know that the threat was still among us and about to pull out the worst in me. From this moment forward, I knew I would no longer operate from the mindset of head of The Table. Mahogany the boss was treacherous, but Mahogany the mother was a motherfucka that would haunt your dreams and wake the dead behind my kid.

Grabbing my gun from underneath the pillow I'd slept on, I quickly traded Justice's basketball shorts for my jeans. Sliding my feet in my shoes, I snatched up my purse from the ottoman in front of his bed and made my way to his bedroom door without so much as a peep.

"Damn, Mama, you just gon' leave without saying bye or hittin' your mouth with some toothpaste?" I heard him say in a playful manner from behind me just as I was a few steps from his door.

I wasn't in a joking mood at all. Not giving myself a second to fully think my next move through, I spun around with my gun raised directly

1

at his head. "Did you lure me here last night and have my kid snatched up?" Taking the gun off safety, silence fell over the room. My eyes turned to slits, and the look of lust I once had was now replaced with deadly fire.

With his eyes never leaving mine, Justice titled his head as if he were examining the gun to see if it was loaded.

"I don't have your kid, Mahogany. I hate to hear that she's even missing." His tone was even, but the anger and offense was there. The crease in his forehead gave it away as well. "While you're standing here having a stare down with me, you should be kicking down doors to find your little one."

"Excuse me?" Now, I was offended and didn't appreciate the condescending tone. My finger rested on the trigger, ready to squeeze.

"Mahogany, if you actually believed that I orchestrated or personally carried out that foul ass shit you just accused me of, you would've squeezed until the clip was empty. So, like I said, instead of having this face off with me, you should be kicking down doors and narrowing down your suspect pool."

My phone rang, and there was a knock at his door at the same time.

"Come in, Ma," he called out, his eyes never leaving mine.

"Hey, I was just... I know damn well..." Her voice trailed off, and I heard the sound of a gun cocking behind me. I wasn't the least bit fazed though. We could have a shootout in this bitch for all I cared. "Now, sweetheart, I'm not sure how you think this is gonna play out, but that young man you're standing in front of is my pride and joy. My heart in human form. From the day he was born, I promised his father that I'd be judged by twelve before I let him be carried by six. I'm sure you catch my drift."

"She's good, Ma." Justice spoke on my behalf. "Put y'all guns down and let me get dressed." He turned, walking away, leaving the two of us standing in the middle of his bedroom.

"I don't have time for this shit. I gotta go find my baby." Just saying the words out loud, my chest tightened, and air felt constricted. About facing, I was face-to-face with his mother.

She was a beautiful, middle-aged woman with rich, caramel colored skin like Justice. Her hair was pulled back from her face in a low ponytail, fully displaying the *fuck around and find out* look she had. I hadn't seen her last night when I arrived, and this wasn't the best introduction for the two of us.

"That ain't no way to show a man you like him, boo. I'm sure Antoinette taught you that. And I know she ain't snag a man of Coolie's stature by being so aggressive."

I didn't bother asking how she knew my mother, nor did I respond to her admiration for my dad. I'd wasted enough time. I needed to locate my child. I went to walk past her, and she put her hand on my arm, stopping me. Glancing down at her hand and back up at her face, she seemed unfazed by my stance.

"I don't know what's going on, but if you need anything, let us know. Me and your parents go way back." After one final look, she let my arm go, and I proceeded to make my exit.

Jumping in my car, I threw my purse in the backseat and sat my gun and phone in my lap. Leaning forward and resting my head on the steering wheel, my heart raced, and all of my emotions came pouring out of me. Hitting the steering wheel a few times, I let out a scream so loud I was sure it could be heard outside of the car. Somebody had my innocent child, and the thought of bodily harm being done to her made the hairs on my neck stand up. I knew I had to shake the emotions; my baby couldn't get my best efforts if I was out moving reckless.

One thing I knew for sure, I was at any and everyone's head until my daughter was back home safe and sound. Everyone's safety was in jeopardy at this point. Inhaling deeply, a full exhale followed as I started my car. Connecting my phone to Bluetooth, I made the command to call Briscoe. Unlike the recent times when I called him, he answered on the first ring.

"What I do now?"

"Meet me at my house. Somebody snatched up Beautii."

"Somebody did what?! What the fuck is you sayin' to me right now, Mahogany?"

"Look, I know just about as much as you right now, Briscoe, which is much of nothing. Just go to my house please. I'm on my way there, so I can figure this shit out."

"You mean so we can figure this shit out. This our mother-fuckin' child you talkin' bout, Hogany. What the fuck, man?!"

"You know what I mean, Briscoe. I ain't got time or fuckin' energy to go back-and-forth witchu about what I'm gon' do or what we gon' do. Let's just DO THIS SHIT, SO WE CAN GET OUR CHILD HOME!" I hit the end button on my steering wheel and shifted the car into drive.

Just as I went to drive off, two knocks at my window halted my push on the gas. Justice stood outside of my car with a facial expression I couldn't read and didn't have time to decode. I opened my mouth to tell him to back up, but before I could, he opened the passenger side door and slid into the seat.

"Time is not on our side. We'll hash that lil' shit out that happened inside at a later date once we find your little one. Just know that it'll be the last time you pull a gun out on me. Drive, Mahogany."

I didn't have it in me to have a war of words with him. Putting my foot on the gas, I mashed out. I was gonna find my child, and when I did, the person who'd taken her, or even had a hand in it, was going to die a slow and painful death that was sure to be whispered about for years.

"What did your daughter have on this morning?" Justice inquired, disturbing the silence I so desperately needed in order to focus and maintain a level head.

"I couldn't tell you. I was too busy laid up witchu when I should've been home being a mother."

"Aye, don't start that *woe is me* shit. That ain't gon' help get her back no faster. You need to continue to be that same boss you've been since the day I met you at my car wash. That's what's going to guarantee your daughter's safe return. When you get to acting on emotions is when shit goes left."

Tears pricked my eyes as he spoke, but I couldn't let them fall. Not because I didn't want to appear weak in front of him, but because tears weren't gonna do anything but piss me off further. I heard everything he said, but I was still overwhelmed with emotions. Being a mother made you both strong and weak at the same time — strong in that God saw fit to place a little human in your care that you'd move Heaven and Earth for and take on any hardship life had to offer just to keep them safe and weak in that parenting made you vulnerable and sometimes caused you to make erratic decisions based on emotions.

It was a tough role yet rewarding at the same time. Still, no matter how I felt at the moment, I knew for shit sure that nobody would sleep until I found Beautii. Just as I turned my car onto my street, my phone rang. A number I didn't recognize flashed on the car's dashboard. Disconnecting the phone from the Bluetooth, I picked it up. I stared at the screen and mentally prepared myself for bullshit. Taking in a deep breath and exhaling slowly, I let the call ring three times before swiping to answer and putting the phone to my ear.

"Hello?"

"Is this Mahogany?" the unknown caller spoke. I couldn't place the male voice, but it was clear he knew me.

"Who is this?" Parking right outside of my house, I kept the ignition running. The caller paused, and I could hear light breathing on the other end of the phone. **"Hello,"** I spoke again, my voice laced with irritation.

"Is this Mahogany?" the caller repeated.

"No, this isn't Mahogany. This is a bitch with little, no scratch that, no patience for this prank call bullshit. Now, you only have seconds to state your business or clear my motherfuckin' line." I'd put so much emphasis on the cuss words, spit flew from my mouth.

Justice tapped my shoulder and held up his phone for me to see. On the screen was his notes app. He typed for me to calm down and put the call on speakerphone. I did, and he kept his phone up next to mine. I could hear shuffling in the background, followed by what sounded like a door being opened.

"Get off me!" Hearing Beautii's voice clear as day, my body went still, and the phone slipped out of my hand, falling in my lap.

Without a second thought, Justice grabbed it and held it up to his mouth. **"How much?"** he asked the caller, taking control.

"Who da fuck is this?"

"That's not important. Give us a number." He was calm and calculating as he spoke.

"**Man, put the woman in charge back on the phone,**" the caller spat.

"**I'm here,**" I spoke through gritted teeth.

"**Good. As you can see, I have something of yours. The last thing I wanna do is hurt your little girl. I actually like kids. I want some of my own someday. I...**"

"**Whatever it is you want, you got it,**" I cut him off. "**Just let me speak to her.**"

"**Oh, my bad. She can hear you.**"

"**I'm here, Mommy. Please, please come get me.**"

I held my hand up to my mouth and bit my finger to contain my anger. "**Beautii, what I always tell you?**"

"**Anything or anyone that tries to come between us will be met with grave consequences.**"

"**That's right, my girl. Mommy coming. Believe that.**"

"**Alright, Colombiana,**" the male voice returned. "**I need 50K. I'll hit you with the details shortly.**" The line went dead.

"Motherfucka!" I screamed out. "I swear I'm gonna kill everybody involved. This bitch ass nigga kidnapped my kid for a measly 50K!" Not only was I seething mad, but I was offended. Fifty thousand dollars didn't even cover the jewelry in Beautii's jewelry box. "Okay, I see how we doing this. Y'all got the right one."

Chapter Two

MORAE

"Aight now, Mo, when we get over here, don't get out this car embarrassing me. The only thing worse than a man and a woman going at it is two lesbians. You better represent the LGBTQIA community right and be civilized. I got all the letters correct, didn't I?" As Tiffany rambled, I swerved in and out of traffic, listening to Waze as it guided us to where the Apple locator said Paris was last.

After dropping Tiff home, I found myself driving around with no destination for hours. Something in my gut told me that wherever Paris was, I needed to get to her. That feeling alone prompted me to call her phone ten times back to back. Each time it went to voicemail, that feeling in my gut got stronger. When I finally made it home to lay it down for the night, sleep was a distant memory. I found myself back at Tiff's house early in the morning. When she saw my face, she got dressed, threw on her coat and shoes, and we were back in my car. Instead of calling Paris again, I tracked her.

She'd started sharing her location with me a while ago, and although I had never thought to track her before, the Apple feature had come in handy today.

"Tiff, the last thing on my mind is beefing with her. I just need to see her face to calm this uneasiness in my stomach. Something ain't right."

"*Have you tried calling her aunt again?*"

I shook my head no. "She called me this morning, but I didn't answer. I don't know what to tell that lady, Tiff. And until I lay my eyes on Paris, I'm not alluding to any information that I don't have."

"*I get that.*" *Waze announced that we'd arrived at our destination after a forty-seven-minute drive.* "*You ready?*"

I nodded, not wanting to admit that I was anything but ready out loud. I thought Tiff knew it too because she didn't push for verbal confirmation. She gave me a minute before we both stepped out with no clue of what we were walking into. I took note of the seedy area we were in and put my hand up to my hip to ensure my Glock 9 was secure underneath my peacoat. Entering the motel, the unpleasant, stale smell of cigarettes polluted the air. Red flag number two. I knew for a fact that Paris wouldn't willingly find herself in a dilapidated motel that looked like it had failed many inspections.

As we pushed forward, toward the front desk, walking on the dingy carpet made me feel like my Prada sneakers deserved better. With no one at the desk, I used the sleeve of my coat to ring the bell. It went unanswered for a few seconds, and that was all it took before Tiff became impatient.

"*Hellooo!*" *she yelled out, hitting the bell a few more times.*

"*Excuse me.*" *A dark skin woman with blue box braids appeared from behind a door labeled office. Her lip was curled up as if we had interrupted something she had going on.* "*You can't be ringing the bell like that.*"

"*Show me a sign that says I can't,*" *Tiff challenged.* "*And then, once you find that sign, find me something that says it's okay for your black ass to not be posted up at this counter to greet customers as they come into this crack shack.*"

The woman sucked her teeth and pulled her long braids back from her face. "*How can I help you?*" *She rolled her eyes hard and put her hand on her hip.*

Navigating the gallery in my phone, I pulled up a picture of Paris and held it up for her to see. "*Did this woman come in here tonight?*" *Squinting her eyes, she leaned forward. The gesture let me know that she was about to lie, so I forewarned her before she did.* "*Listen, the woman in this picture is very important to me. Before you think of a lie to tell, please understand that I will shoot this lobby up, and the first bullet will hit your chest before anything." I watched as she swallowed hard and stared at me through scared eyes. "Did you see her?"*

"Y... ye... yes. Room 412. She came in with a man. I'll give you the key." Without hesitation, she turned and reached behind her into a drawer. Pulling out a red and white key card, she handed it to me.

"Thank you."

She nodded.

"Stop shaking," Tiff let out. "Shaking tells me that you'll probably be on the phone with the cops as soon as we leave, and that's a no go, feel me?"

"You got my word." The girl attempted to assure Tiff with a less than sure response.

With my phone still in my hand, I snapped a picture of her. "And now we have your face. Don't play wit your life. Room 412, right?"

"Room 412," she reconfirmed. Gesturing with my head for Tiff to come on, we both about faced. "The elevators are down the hall and to your right."

We followed her directions, and the lights seemed to dim as we walked farther down the hall.

"The only way I can see someone staying at this hole in the wall is if they tryna be ducked off. I know my girl, P, ain't come here willingly." Tiff spoke her thoughts out loud, making me pause and reach for her arm, halting her steps. She turned to me and gave me a confident nod. "I got you." Her reassurance was needed for me to keep pressing forward.

Taking the elevator up to the fourth floor, we followed the arrows on the wall to room 412. Outside the door, I went to insert the keycard and stopped just before the light could change, granting us access. With my eyes straight ahead, I spoke.

"Tiff, I'm scared that whatever is behind this door is going to break me. I'm no good to anyone broken." My heart rate quickened. My mind had already concluded that whatever was on the other side of the door wasn't good.

Placing her hand over mine, she pushed the key in the door, and it clicked. Entering the room behind Tiff, I took note of the silence, and the same stale smell from the lobby was apparent, but the smell of blood outweighed that. I felt the aching in my chest just as Tiff stopped short and hung her head.

"Damn," she whispered, moving to the side for me to see.

"Nooo, P. Please, Paris. Please don't do this shit to me." My voice cracked as I continued to walk toward the chair that she was bound to. Her head was slumped over, and I could see dried up blood on her shirt.

"You can't, Mo," Tiff let out as I went to pick up Paris' head.

I averted my eyes to her and broke. "I have to, Tiffany. I have to see her face."

"Mo, you can't touch her."

"Don't you think I know that?!" I snapped in a low growl to avoid bringing attention to the room.

"Okay," she responded softly.

"I..."

"It's okay, sis. I understand."

Sniffling, I kneeled down in front of Paris. I understood what Tiff said about me not touching her body to avoid leaving my prints, so I used my sleeve to touch her leg.

"I love you, P. I love you, and I'm gonna make damn sure that the person responsible for this shit pays with their life. On everything I love, I'ma make them pay."

<hr>

"What she say?" Tiff asked as I hung up with Mahogany and laid back on the headrest in the passenger seat.

I was in no shape to drive. It didn't even feel like I was present. I was numb. Tears cascaded freely down my cheeks, and my chest tightened. After vowing to find whoever had taken Paris' life, we had to make a swift exit. I couldn't bring myself to leave her body in the rundown motel alone though. After having Tiff put in an anonymous call about a dead body in the room, we stayed until EMS arrived.

I couldn't bring myself to call Paris' aunt just yet, so I called Hogany. When her voice came through the phone, I broke. Paris was gone. Someone had taken her from me. Even worse than that, someone had taken her from her son in the most violent way. What hurt more than the fact that I wasn't there to stop it from happening was knowing that it had to do with her association with me. There was nothing anyone could tell me that Paris had done to warrant a bullet to the head. This shit was personal and had everything to do with my seat at The Table.

"She put me on hold, and the call dropped. Tiff, they killed my baby. Shot her in the fuckin' head! She was executed. And for what, cause a motherfucka didn't have the balls to come at me directly? They gon' feel it, Tiffany. I swear to God!" I hit the dashboard twice and threw my phone up against it.

"We gon' make it right, Mo. We gon' make it right." Tiff pressed her lips tightly together, and I watched as they trembled. Her hands gripped the steering wheel tightly as she kept her eyes glued to the road.

I could tell she was suppressing her own emotions to accommodate mine. Like Hogany, she'd accepted Paris and had grown to love her too. I knew that her declaration to make it right for Paris was solid. My phone rang from the floor, indicating that it didn't take a hard enough hit to the dashboard to damage it. Picking it up, the screen showed an incoming call from Paris' aunt. As her number danced across the screen, I grimaced, finding it hard to accept that I would have to be the one to break the news. I couldn't handle being the bearer of bad news that I was still trying to process myself, so I declined the call.

"You want me to take you home, or did you want to go to her aunt's house? I can stay with you."

"That was her aunt who just called. I can't bring myself to share the news. I'm gonna call Hogany back and see if she can take care of it. I…"

"You don't have to answer right this moment, but she needs to hear the news from you, Mo. Hogany was close to her, but it was the two of you who were building a life together. Her family needs to hear it from you, especially her son."

I diverted my eyes from hers and turned to look out the window. Again, she was right. My thoughts went to Paris' son. DJ was her world, and as a packaged deal, he became my heart just as she had. Having to tell him that he wouldn't see his mother again made my heart ache. My pain would never compare to his, but I planned to ensure that he knew that he always had me. At only two, his mind wouldn't be able to register grief, but he'd know loss without his mother.

My phone rang again, and this time, it was Dudas calling. I wanted to ignore his call too, but his calling meant he had information.

"Yeah, Dudas."

"Go straight home and don't make any detours. I'll meet you there in an hour."

"What do you know?"

He sighed. **"Please just get house and we'll talk once I get there."**

"Alright, Dudas," I replied with no energy to go back-and-forth.

"Sis, I'm sorry about Pa..."

"Thanks, bruh," I cut him off. **"I gotta go."** Ending the call, I set the phone in my lap.

Tiffany held her hand out to me, and I placed my hand in hers. Giving it a reassuring squeeze, she repeated that she had me.

"Bae, do you have life insurance?" Paris asked, looking up from where she lay on my chest.

It was two in the morning, and we'd just finished raiding my snack cabinet. She had a sweet tooth and would often wake up in the middle of the night just doing shit. Tonight, she included me in her big back activities.

My eyes narrowed, and my lips pressed into a thin line as I studied her with a gaze that was both curious and confused as to why she would ask such a question so randomly. "Yeah, I have life insurance. Why? You plottin' to take me out for Monk Man or something? He's the sole beneficiary."

With a tight face, she sat up straight. "Don't even play with me like that, Morae. That's not even funny."

"I'm not playing. Why you ask?"

"I don't know. I've been thinking a lot about death lately. And before you go saying something stupid, don't. I am not tryna take you out. I would never dream of bringing you harm. I've been thinkin' a lot about... my death. When it's my time to go, I want to make sure that DJ is straight. You know I don't come from a big family, and the closest person to me is my aunt, Reece. There's my mom too, but you know the situation with that."

"I don't know why you've been thinking about death, but I understand where you're coming from. Just know that if anything were to ever happen

to you, DJ will forever be straight. And while you know that, understand that so long as I have breath in my body, no harm will come to you or him."

A tear trickled down her face that I didn't see coming. "Neither one of us can say when it's time for us to go. But, when the time comes for me, I just want to know that my son will continue to be loved and protected. I also need you to promise me something."

"What's that?" I didn't want to speak on the death topic much longer, but it seemed important for her to get it off her chest, so I listened.

"Promise me that you'll remain in DJ's life and make sure he never forgets me."

"I promise."

The car came to a full stop in front of my building, pulling me from the flashback I had of a conversation I had with Paris a few weeks ago. While I wasn't able to keep my promise and save her, I was determined to keep my word when it came to being there for DJ and keeping her memory alive. As the silence in the car reached a deafening point, the ringing of Tiffany's phone was a welcomed distraction. Grabbing the phone from the cup holder, she held the screen up for me to see the incoming call from Mahogany. Swiping her hand across the screen to answer, she placed the call on speakerphone.

"Where y'all at?" Hogany inquired once the call connected. The urgency in her voice made me sit up straight.

"We just pulled up to Mo's place. Hogany, shit is all..."

"I need y'all here. Somebody snatched Beautii. I don't know much other than a call I got demanding 50K for her return. I need..." She paused, and her sniffling made me uneasy.

Mahogany didn't cry. Her crying signified defeat to me, and that was something we couldn't have.

"Say what now?" Tiffany inquired.

"We're on our way." I spoke up and gestured for Tiff to start the car.

"Thank y'all so much. I'm really trying my best not to lose my shit. This my baby, y'all. This Beautii."

"Our baby that we're going to get back," Tiffany corrected and declared. **"I don't wanna hear nothing else you gotta say unless it's that, Mahogany."**

I nodded in agreement. As they continued to talk, I sent a message to Dudas that I wouldn't be home if he came looking for me. I added that I needed him to notify Paris' aunt of her passing. I didn't have the words to speak but would be sure to reach out once I had the strength to if she didn't call me first.

"Mo," Hogany called out to me.

"Yes?"

"We're gonna find the person responsible for what happened to Paris."

"No doubt about it," I replied. **"Let's focus on what we can fix at the moment. Beautii is out there waiting for us. We need to get to her and soon. See you in a minute."**

We'd lost Paris; I'd be damned if we had the same result with Beautii. We were gonna find my niece alive and well. We couldn't catch a break around this motherfucka. Whoever was working against us had surely hit us hard, but we wouldn't be down for long. For now, my mourning would have to take a backseat. I had to turn up my savage.

"You think we're being tested?" Tiffany questioned Hogany, pulling a deep sigh from her.

"I don't know, Tiff, but the next twenty-four hours is critical. I don't know what I'm liable to do if I don't see my child's face within that timeframe."

Her pain could be felt through the phone, only fueling the revenge in me. She was right. This shit was critical. And I was gonna see to it that we didn't lose another one of ours.

Chapter Three

TIFFANY

I GRIPPED THE STEERING WHEEL TIGHTLY AS I NAVIGATED the streets of Manhattan to hop on the highway, enroute to Hogany's. My eyes were fixed on the road, but my mind was elsewhere. The feeling that the worst hadn't hit us yet plagued my thoughts. Mo may not have sensed it, but holding her hand wasn't just for her comfort but mine too. I'd seen plenty of bodies and had been responsible for a few, but to see someone innocent like Paris, who I'd grown to love, get caught up was a lot for me. Now to find out Beautii was missing, my head was all over the place. And to add insult to injury, my chest had been aching since I left the house this morning.

I'd refused the pain medication from Money yesterday because I hated how it made me feel. With it being my first day back, I needed to be coherent and on point. I had to be there for my girls. While I shared in their pain, I wasn't in their shoes. Silently coaching myself to be prepared for anything at this point, I pushed the pain to the back of my mind.

"Beautii's kidnapping and Paris' death are linked together. I can feel it in my gut, Tiff. I know I'm not wrong."

"What makes you say that?" Turning onto Mahogany's street, I slowed the car down as we approached her house.

"Think about it. This shit is happening back to back. Whoever is orchestrating this shit, their goal is to get to those closest to us in an attempt to cripple us emotionally. And the way to do that is by going through the family."

Nodding, I agreed but still had questions. "I can see that, but why kill Paris? If it's them trying to go after family, why not go after Monk Man since he's the baby of your family?"

"You can't just get to Monk Man. Paris was an easy target. And whether you wanna believe it or not, I left her open to be one, a fuck up that I'll always regret."

Typing in the gate code, we drove up Mahogany's driveway where I noticed three cars along with her Tesla parked out front. I recognized Goddy's Mercedes and my father's Charger, but the blue Toyota Corolla looked out of place amongst the foreign cars. Mo hopped out first, and I followed suit, jogging up the steps and to the door. As Mo went to ring the bell, the door opened to Santana on the other side of it along with the woman he was with the first night I met him.

His eyes lingered on Mo's, and I took note of the subtle spark in them. His attempt to restrain his wandering eye failed, and it was clear that his woman picked up on it as well. The clearing of her throat prompted Santana to speak.

"Wassup, y'all? This is..."

"Don't give a fuck," Mo cut him off. "Excuse me." Pushing the door open wide enough to enter, she breezed past the two and into the house.

"Let me talk to you for a minute, Santana."

I had never spoken to him one on one, and this was the best time to do so considering the situation at hand. As far as I was concerned, everyone outside of our immediate circle, which consisted of us and our parents, was a suspect.

Given his sudden appearance, he was at the top of my list of people I needed to keep my eye on. Nodding, he whispered something in his woman's ear, to which she shot me a jealous scowl before making her way down the steps. It was a small thing that I couldn't feed into. An insecure bitch would always feel the need to be extra territorial, especially with a nigga as friendly as Santana portrayed himself to be.

"Aight, wassup?"

"Do you have any beef in Cali that could've followed you here?"

"Nah, I don't. In case you didn't know, I'm fresh out of state custody not even a month. I ain't got shit going on that would warrant any heat to this magnitude."

Keeping my eyes dead locked on him, I nodded. "Okay."

"Look, I just went through this interrogation with Coolie and your pops. And just like I told them, y'all might view me as an outsider, but I ain't. I wanna find my niece too."

"Coolie?" I questioned, confused.

"Yeah. He's inside."

That was news to me. I had no clue that my godfather was home. "For your sake, Santana, I hope none of this shit ties to you. You don't wanna be on the other side of The Table. Take one of ours, I'ma need all of yours."

Leaving him to fully think on what I said, I entered the house and headed straight to the living room where I heard everyone gathered. My mother sat on the couch with Goddy while my father and Coolie stood on the other side of the room in deep conversation. Just as I went to speak, Coolie turned in my direction.

"Wassup, gangsta?" Flashing his signature smile, he walked over to me with his arms outstretched.

"It's good to have you home." I embraced him and sighed.

"It's good to be back. And we'll celebrate my homecoming soon. Right now, I need us all on one accord. Hogany, Mo, I need everyone to gather around. Dough, get Santana for me."

My dad kissed my forehead and walked past me to the door. Seconds later, he returned with Santana. Mahogany, Mo, and surprisingly, Justice walked from the opposite direction. Hogany hadn't mentioned that he was present when we spoke on the phone. As we gathered around, he stood a few steps back, behind Mahogany. Noting the protective gesture, I listened as Coolie spoke.

"I need y'all to listen to me and listen very clear. Our family is under attack, and the opposition has hit us in a major way. Our main objective is to find Beautii and bring her home safely without a hair out of place nor a wrinkle in her clothes. Killing the motherfucka responsible for this shit will happen immediately after. Understand that I don't care about the why. All I care about is getting my grandbaby back. That said, any enemies you may have made, any people you may have wronged, I need to know a full rundown of who they are. I don't give a fuck if we gotta kick in every door in New York State, Beautii will be found."

Every word he spoke, I felt, and as each person went down the line, giving an account of their run ins over the last month, I'd come to the consensus that we didn't have many enemies. That alone would make it harder to track down who had Beautii. There was no doubt in my mind that it would be done though. Everyone outside of the room we stood in was a suspect and would be treated as such until Beautii was back with us.

Hogany had yet to speak, but her silence was loud. I could only imagine what was going through her head at the moment. Her only child, the child she'd carried in her body and promised to protect with her life, had been kidnapped. I was gonna do everything in my power to bring back her peace.

"Hogany, what you thinking?" I asked, causing her to glance in my direction.

"I'm thinking about this bullshit ass ransom they asked for. Why 50K? Clearly, they know whose child they took, so they gotta know that $50,000 is pocket change to a bitch like me."

"You think there's something else going on?"

"It gotta be. I gotta figure this shit out and quick."

"Aye," Coolie called out to her. "Now is not the time to be thinking about going on no solo missions, Mahogany. We in this shit together. Every last one of us."

"I hear you, Dad." Though Mahogany nodded her understanding of what Coolie had said, we all knew that she was going to do whatever she deemed necessary whether it included the collective or not.

The doorbell chimed, pulling all of our attention. My father went to answer it, returning with an angry Briscoe who barely spoke to any of us before he made a beeline to Mahogany.

"What the fuck happened?! And why it seems like I'm the last one to find out about **my** missing kid? Y'all in here all huddled up and shit."

I went to check him about his tone at the same time as Mahogany, but Coolie stepped in.

"Aye, Briscoe, I know you ain't turn blind out this bitch while I was away, so I'ma need you to chill the fuck out with all that base in your tone. I understand that you are just as concerned as we are about your baby but don't get put on your fuckin' neck walkin' up on mine like that."

"Coolie, you know I respect you and all, but this **my** child we talkin' bout, and I need answers."

"Excuse me, Mr. Iwannabeafatherwhenitsconvient lately but it's **our** child who's out there, okay?" Mahogany let out.

"Oh, yeah? Well, tell me this. Where were you when **our** child went missing?" He questioned her as if she were on trial. Mahogany went silent and dropped her head. "And who is this nigga?" He pointed at Justice who'd moved closer, positioning himself directly behind Mahogany.

"I'm the nigga that put holes in overly emotional ass niggas like you," Justice spoke up. "But since there's a more pressing matter at hand, I'll hold off."

"Nigga, wh..." Briscoe went to speak but was cut off by Goddy.

"Hey! I don't give a flying fuck if y'all niggas shoot each other to death; it will be **after** my grandbaby is found. Now, get y'all shit together, come up with a plan, and execute. The more time we spend lookin' at each other, the less time we're putting into finding her."

"She's right," I added, turning to Briscoe. "Where she was when everything went down is irrelevant. What we know is Beautii was kidnapped by someone looking to get at us."

"Look, I'm trying to figure out what happened to my daughter. I think asking the whereabouts of her mother is valid."

"I wasn't here. I didn't come home last night," Mahogany shamefully admitted. "What else you wanna know?"

"Let me guess, you had better things to do than be a mother to our child," he spat, cutting his eyes over at Justice.

He was so callous in his words, the whole room got quiet.

"Briscoe, lemme talk to you outside," Coolie demanded, walking over to Briscoe and turning him around.

"Yeah, outside is where he betta go cause in a minute, I'ma forget we created Beautii together and his people gon' be looking for him."

Hogany spat venom. The threat lingered in the air as Coolie and my father walked Briscoe to the door.

"This shit is crazy," I spoke. "We gotta move as one, and the parents at each other's throats ain't gon' bring Beautii back any faster," I reasoned with facts.

The remaining people in the room murmured their agreement, but Mahogany's face remained stoic. Justice shrugged his shoulders, giving off a feel that he was down for whatever, and that was the energy we needed. Briscoe, Coolie, and my father reentered the living room with Briscoe still cutting his eyes at Justice. The tension in the air was thick for sure.

"Is there anyone on your side that we need to be looking into, Briscoe? Any new beef we need to know about?" Coolie questioned.

"Nah. No one that would have done no shit like this. When I'm in some shit, I keep it far away from the family. Any of y'all think to question Mahogany's new nigga?"

"He has nothing to do with this. And if I'm vouching for him, there's nothing else that needs to be said on the matter," Mahogany stated clearly. "This has everything to do with The Table."

There was no disputing that Beautii's kidnapping and Paris' death had everything to do with The Table. I only hoped that the people involved were fully aware of what they stepped into.

Chapter Four

SANTANA

I PLAYED THE BACKGROUND, LISTENING AS EVERYONE SPOKE, giving their input on what move to make next. I wanted to step in to say something but knew my timing had to be right. The way Tiff had approached me outside let me know that although I was now a part of The Table, they still had me on a trial run. Beautii being kidnapped had caught me off guard, especially with it going down at my mom's house. If I knew anything, there was no way Coolie would leave her easily accessible, so someone snatching Beautii up from their home was odd.

"If I may," I went to speak, and all eyes shifted in my direction. Renee, who had returned from outside, grabbed me by the back of my shirt as I stepped forward. Turning slightly, I nodded that I was good. "I think the problem is the suspect pool is too large. In the business we're in, we make an enemy every day. Even those we least expect."

"You mean like you?" Mahogany uttered, mugging me. "We **been** in this business, running shit with no problem. Shit been cool. Any issues deaded along with the issuer before it even became something we couldn't control. And then, ol' cool ass Santana comes in town, and all of a sudden, things go from sugar to shit. Make that make sense."

"So, what you tryna say? You ain't gotta beat around the bush. Say that shit straight up."

"Ain't nobody beating around no fuckin' bush. I'm tellin' you none of this shit started happening until you brought yo ass back around. And you better hope don't none of this tie back to you in no way. I could give a fuck about us being blood."

"Alright now, Mahogany." My mother stepped in between us. "You taking this shit too far. That is your brother!"

I watched her stare our mother down before diverting her eyes to me. They told me everything I needed to know. That sibling shit didn't mean anything to her when it came down to it. And while my initial intention was to do anything in my power to take her seat as boss, her child, my niece, being kidnapped was nowhere a part of the plan. Kids were off limits in my book, no matter who they were.

"Check it out, feel how you wanna feel about me as a man and hell, even as a brother, but know that at the end of the day, I'm a father. And all this other bullshit you poppin' aside, Beautii is my niece. I'ma help you look for her regardless of how you feel, Mahogany."

With her face unwavering, she doubled down on her feelings. "I said what I said."

"Y'all done beefing?" Coolie spoke, pinching the bridge of his nose. "Cause quite frankly, that's all the fuck y'all been doing since we've been here. Do I gotta sit everyone the fuck down and do this shit myself?" No one uttered a word. "Aight then, I don't wanna hear shit else unless it has to do with a plan and execution. Now, Santana, I need for you to get your daughter and your lady and take them back to the house, so we can keep an eye on them until we figure this shit out."

"You mean the same house Beautii was snatched from?" Renee interjected. "Yeah, no. We don't have anything to do with what's going on, so we'll take our chances at the hotel. I'm tryna keep my baby safe."

Before anyone could respond, Mahogany sidestepped me and my mother and yoked Renee up.

"Fuck you say, bitch? You tryna say I can't protect my fuckin' daughter? Who the fuck gon' protect you and stop me from squeezing the life from yo body? Huh, bitch? Tell me that since you got so much to say."

"Mahogany, what the fuck, man?!" I went to grab her hand and heard guns cocking behind me.

"We'll take this search party from eleven to nine real quick," Tiffany spoke calmly with her gun pointed at my head.

Out of the corner of my eye, I could see Morae, who had been quiet since arriving, with her gun up, while everyone stood around, waiting for it to go down. Inside, my blood was boiling, not because I was outnumbered but because yet again, I was made to feel like an outcast.

"Let my girl go, Mahogany."

"Mahogany, let her go now," Coolie demanded.

After a lingering hold for a few more seconds, she let up, and Renee hit the floor, coughing, with tears falling from her eyes. Helping her up, I shook my head.

"This shit crazy. Here we are, tryna help out, and this is the shit you pull? Y'all gon stop tryna play me like I'm some duck ass nigga!" I barked, fed the fuck up.

"I'm ready to go!" Renee yelled out from the side of me. "These people don't give a fuck about you, Santana! And they for damn sure don't care about me or Asia if they acting like this." Her voice was full of emotion, and I just hoped that she didn't start crying. There was absolutely no room for that shit right now. "Come on, Santana," she pulled at my arm, "let's go."

"This is fucking crazy. Put y'all guns down. Nobody is going anywhere." My mother stepped in once again. "Renee, I understand your concern, trust me I do, and the fact that this happened in my home has me uneasy too, but being with us is your safest choice right now."

I could tell she was trying to reason, but I didn't like how she wasn't calling Mahogany out on her bullshit. While a part of me understood her frustration, she was taking that shit out on the wrong people.

"I'm out," Renee announced.

"Yeah, cause the safest place you can be right now is the fuck up outta here," Mahogany chastised.

"Man, we ain't going nowhere," I said, grabbing Renee's hand before she could walk away. "Now, we may not be welcome in your home, but if **our** mama say we can be in hers, then that's where we'll be. You not bout to keep violating my woman though. It's enough of that shit."

"I know one thing," Coolie interjected, "y'all both got thirty seconds to back down before I get to clicking out. You two," he pointed to me and Renee, "stand in that corner, and Hogany, you go in that one."

Our respective corners, where we now both stood stone faced, were only a couple feet away from each other.

"And neither one of y'all better move unless I give the go ahead. Now, Hogany, you said you got a call when you pulled up. What was said? Was there any distinct background noises or anything that stuck out to you? I need to know the entire conversation again down to the sound of the person's voice."

Mahogany ran down the call once more, giving every detail, describing the voice on the call as best she could. "That's all I got, Daddy. But I can't stand around here too much longer. I gotta make a move."

"I'm ready to go," Renee whispered through gritted teeth.

"I'm gonna drop her off, then I'll be right back. I'm ridin' out with y'all 'bout this. I don't care how anybody feels about it. Coolie, keep me posted if y'all move before I get back."

He nodded, and I caught Mahogany roll her eyes.

"I'll get Asia," my mom offered with sad eyes before walking back to the room where Asia had been since we arrived.

I knew Renee wanted to protest, but I signaled for her to be cool. My mother walked back out with Asia, who seemed oblivious to the tension in the air, but I knew better. Unlike Renee, who battled to maintain control of her emotions, I was teaching Asia to never let how she felt be displayed on her face when she was in a tight situation.

"I'll be back," I assured my mother as I took Asia's hand.

She gave me a weak smile in return, and we walked out.

"I don't know what kind of fucked up need you got to be a part of that shit back there, but this is not what I came here for. This is the second time your sister has violated us, and now this bitch done put her hands on me! Hell no! The Wright family got me fucked up!" Renee expressed as soon as she closed the passenger side door. "Me and Asia can go right back to Cali and deal with my dysfunctional ass family for all this."

This was exactly what the fuck I didn't need. I had a plan that I wanted to see through. With Coolie back, and me helping get Beautii back, it would be another step toward me getting that head seat.

"I hear you but leaving is not an option. Let me deal with my people. Yes, my sister goes too far, but under the circumstances, I'm inclined to give her a pass. Her daughter is missing. You would be losing yo shit if it was ours. Yes, she was dead ass wrong for putting her hands on you, and that shit will be addressed again. But on some real shit, you were dead ass wrong for what you said. You can't control how someone reacts when they feel disrespected."

As expected, she didn't have a rebuttal. She knew she was wrong, but it also didn't make Mahogany right. She had to understand that at the end of the day, I was doing what I had to do for our family. I couldn't just say fuck it and return home to the same shit. I wanted bigger and better for my family, and we were going to have it. I needed her to thug this shit out. She remained quiet for the rest of the ride to the hotel, and once we arrived, she hopped out quick, slamming the door behind her.

"Text me when y'all find Beautii, Dad," Asia said before leaning forward to kiss my cheek.

"I will. I love you, kid."

"I love you too."

I waited until they were inside the building before pulling off and heading back to Mahogany's crib. I had to move smart because this shit was getting tricky, and I had to come out on top.

Chapter Five

RAZOR

As I drove down the street with the little girl bound and gagged in the trunk of my car, I shook my head at the turn of events. My contact let me know I needed to lay low and await further instructions after I was able to successfully snatch her up. That was obvious. I hadn't met the Mahogany chick in person, but from what I'd heard about her in the streets, I knew she would stop at nothing to find her kid, so I had to move like a ghost. I had people in the city, but I couldn't trust a soul with what I had going on right now.

I drove around aimlessly, trying to figure out my next move. I knew I couldn't take her to a hotel. I needed some place discreet. Just as I went to pull over on a residential street to come up with a plan, the gas light came on. I'd been driving around so long in deep thought, the last thing on my mind was running out of gas. A nigga had skipped Kidnapping 101. I wasn't familiar with the area, and with it being dark as hell and quiet, paranoia started to kick in.

I was a Black man, in a tinted-out Lexus LS, with a child in the trunk. I needed to get the fuck on asap. Pulling out my phone, I asked Siri for directions to the nearest gas station. When she responded that there was one a mile out, I glanced at the fuel meter and was confident that I could make it without having to result to pushing. Driving the designated thirty miles per hour, I made it to the gas station without incident. Making sure my LA Dodgers fitted cap was low enough to cover my eyes, I threw my hoodie over my head and exited the car.

As I approached the door to enter the store, I noticed a line forming. Glancing back at the car, I shook my head. There was no way I was leaving it unattended for that long, so I entered cooly and walked to the front of the line. Approaching the woman who was next in line, I pulled out two twenty-dollar bills.

"Wassup, love? You think you can do me a solid and put twenty on pump six? I'm on a time constraint, and I can't do the line. I got a dub for you."

Turning her head to check out the line, she turned back to me. "Where the dub?" she questioned with her hand on her hip.

I held up both twenties, and she smiled.

"Pump six, right?"

"Yes, love. Twenty on the petro and twenty for you. Thank you."

"Mmhmm."

The store clerk called for the next customer, and she switched her thick ass up to the register. The dog in me wanted to admire her walk a little longer, but I was pressed for time. Jogging back over to the car, I pumped the gas while simultaneously searching Goggle for an available Airbnb. I needed somewhere cheap to lay my head for the night. Finding a small single-family home in Staten Island, I booked it, figuring it would be the perfect spot. In my haste, I didn't notice that the shit wouldn't be available until four the next day.

"Goddamn!" I yelled out, slamming the pump back into the holder.

"Hey, you good?" I looked up to see shorty from the store walking in my direction.

"Yeah. Preciate your help."

Licking her lips, she went to speak again. "No problem. What you bout to get into?"

Catching her drift, I replied. "Any other day, it would be you, but I'm in traffic, love. Shoot me your number and a name?" I posed my request as a question.

"Yeah. I can do that." She rattled off her number, and I nodded. "You not gonna write it down?" she questioned with her lip turned up.

I chuckled. "Don't have to. I committed it to memory already, Nia. The name and that ass." I repeated the number back, and she smiled.

"Call soon. I won't be in town for long."

I watched as she switched off, hopped inside an Acura TL, and slowly pulled off. The banging coming from my trunk caught my attention, quickly bringing me back to my reality. Getting in on the driver's side, I left the gas station. Wanting to be close to the Airbnb, I made my way to Staten Island. Sleeping in the car was out of the question, and although I had technically kidnapped the little girl, I couldn't subject her to sleeping in the trunk. With no other options, I found the nearest motel to hold us over for the night. Pulling into the parking lot of a Super 8, I made sure to park far off from the few cars so that I could let her out of the trunk.

Figuring it would be best to pay for the room before letting her out, I made my way inside. My eyes scoped the lobby, checking for any cameras, and landed on the front desk where an Indian man sat with his arms crossed, watching a small TV. He didn't acknowledge my presence until I walked over and hit the counter.

"Aye," I called out.

"How can I help you?" he questioned, never looking my way, his accent thick.

"I need a room for the night."

"It's sixty dollars, plus tax. Are you using cash or card?"

"Cash," I replied, reaching into my pocket and pulling out four twenties. "You can keep the change."

That got him to turn around and flash a yellow smile. "Thank you. Room number four on the first floor."

He handed me a key attached to a small green keychain with a white number four printed on it. Thanking him, I turned to go back to my car and stopped short to grab something for the kid out of the vending machine. It was the only thing in the whole lobby that looked new. Inserting a $10 bill, I got two bags of chips, a Sprite, and a bag of M&M's. Normal kid shit. Placing the items in my hoodie, I took my change and walked back out to my car and around to the trunk.

Shorty was too tall for me to try to carry and play it off like she was my overgrown daughter who was tired from the drive, so a threat to her life to keep her in line would have to do. I went to pop the trunk, and to my surprise, she was wide awake and staring dead at me. She didn't have the eyes of a young kid. There was a fire in them that a killer like myself could respect.

"I'm going to untie you and take the gag off your mouth. When we go in this place, you keep your eyes straight ahead and don't speak. I'm the dad, and you're the punished pre-teen whose phone I just took. Act like that without making a sound. You make a sound or try to run, I send a piece of you back to ya mom. Cool?"

Pulling the .40 from my waist, I held it up for her to see. She nodded slowly. Confident that we were on the same page, I took off the gag first and then untied her legs. Helping her out, I glanced down at her attire. She had on a silk pajama set and a pair of fuzzy slippers. I didn't know how I was going to pull this shit off, but I knew I had to. Grabbing a hoodie from the trunk, I placed it over her, making sure it was up on her head.

"Aight, come on." I held out my hand, and to my surprise, she took it, and we walked into the motel, past the Indian dude who was preoccupied with the TV, and over to the elevators.

As if it were alerted to our presence, the elevator doors opened once we were in front of them. Stepping on, I used my sleeve to press for the first floor. Everything about the motel was rundown, and by the look on the little girl's face, I could tell she had the same thoughts. Reaching the first floor, the elevator doors hesitated before opening. *This is some bullshit,* I thought to myself while escorting shorty over to room four.

Placing the key into the lock, I opened the room door, and the strong smell of mold hit my nose instantly. The room was small with two twin beds, a small TV that set atop a scratched wooden dresser, and a chair that set in the corner. The cracked walls were covered in chipped pale white paint, and I caught two roaches convening near the bathroom.

"This is disgusting," she said, speaking for the first time.

"Yeah, it is. Gotta make the best of it though, lil' one. You take the bed, and I'ma post ip in this chair." Grabbing the chair, I placed it in front of the door. "You hungry?"

She shook her head no.

"Aight, well, if you get hungry, this was all they had in the vending machine." I tossed the chips, soda, and candy on the bed. "I'ma have to put these on you too. I'll leave your mouth uncovered so long as you don't scream."

I used zip ties to tie her hands and feet. Placing her upright so that her back was against the headboard, I tried to make her as comfortable as I could under the circumstances. Taking a step back, I could see tears pooling in the corners of her eyes that she was trying her best to fight back. I didn't have anything to say that would console her. She was just a child caught up in some adult shit unfortunately. I couldn't say things would be alright because shit could really go either way. The only thing I knew was that I couldn't bring myself to kill no kid, so that she didn't have to worry about.

Picking up the remote from the dresser, I sat down on the chair and turned on the TV to drown out the silence in the room. Before I knew it, the TV was watching me.

I AWOKE SEVERAL HOURS LATER, CURSING MYSELF FOR falling asleep like a fucking amateur. Looking over on the bed, I could see she had fallen asleep as well. I found that odd. She hadn't screamed or even tried to escape. Oddly, I couldn't tell if it was due to fear or if she knew something I didn't. Standing, I went over to the dingy curtains to peek out the window. The sun had come up. Pulling my phone from my pocket, I saw that it was a little after seven in the morning. My stomach growled, reminding me that I hadn't eaten since the day before.

I had been so busy on back to back missions, food was the last thing on my mind. I couldn't wait until we were able to check into the Airbnb. Although it appeared ducked off, being in the motel made me feel exposed. Sighing, I walked into the semi clean bathroom to relieve myself. I made sure to leave the door cracked enough to where I could see Beautii, but she couldn't see me. Finishing up, I went to wash my hands. I wanted to wash my face but seeing that the washcloths were as dingy as the curtains on the windows, I opted out.

"Can you untie my hands, so I can eat?" Beautii asked as I exited the bathroom.

"Nah, you good. I tied yo hands up like that for a reason. You gotta make it work, lil' one."

She sighed in defeat, looking down at the bag of Lay's barbeque chips. Picking them up, she maneuvered her hands as best she could to open them. She struggled for a few seconds before figuring it out. Nodding, I went to check my phone, and there was a message from my contact.

> Money Move: How shit going with the kid? Where y'all at?

> Me: At this trash ass motel, just tryna lay low. I got another place for us to go to later this afternoon.

> Money Move: Cool, just stay outta sight. That little girl you got is the key to everything we want. Your next step will be to call Mahogany. Let her know you got her daughter, and you want 50K for her safe return. She'll pay whatever to get that lil crumb snatcher back.

> Me: I hear you, and she definitely gon' pay it, but we lowballing ourselves asking for that pocket change. Especially when we know any amount we tell her, she gon' pay.

> Money Move: I got a plan. Just call her and tell her exactly what I said. I'll be in touch soon.

Scratching my head, I sat back on the chair, staring at the wall. I was already taking a huge risk holding Beautii captive; I damn sure wasn't taking it for no 50K. After several moments of going back-and-forth with myself, I decided to trust my contact and made the call.

"My mama gonna kill you," Beautii spoke with conviction.

"Not if I kill you first," I threatened with a sinister smile, dialing the number I had for Mahogany.

The call didn't go as planned, but I figured by now her people had gathered to find Beautii. After making my demand known, I placed a call to Renee. She'd vowed that when I needed her, she'd be there. She wanted to be my rider; now was the time to put that to the test. The phone rang once before I was sent to voicemail. That only meant Santana was close by, so I sent a text, letting her know that I needed her. Bitches loved to feel needed, so I knew it wouldn't be long before she responded. It was all a waiting game now.

Chapter Six

MAHOGANY

"What exactly did the caller say?" Briscoe asked, looking over at me. He'd finally calmed down enough to speak to me like he had some sense.

"Briscoe, me repeating what was said over and over again is not gonna change anything. Some bum ass nigga called my phone, begging for a bum ass 50K ransom for our daughter."

Hearing myself repeat the same thing out loud was only frustrating me and not helping the situation at all. I understood that everyone wanted answers, but what I wanted was my child in my arms. I needed to hold her, kiss her, and let her know how much Mommy loved her. I needed to admit that I fucked up by not protecting her enough. I didn't give a fuck what we had to do so long as the end result was Beautii back home.

"And I hear you," Briscoe replied. "I'm just tryna make sense of all this shit." He put his head in his hands.

"Well, can we make sense of it while we're out there looking around? I feel like I'm sitting on my hands right now. The longer I sit, the longer our baby is out there, and God knows what is happening."

That constricted feeling in my chest crept up on me, and before I could start to hyperventilate, my eyes found Justice's. He gave a simple head nod and mouthed the words *in and out*. Taking his advice, I breathed in deeply and released the breath slowly. I could hear Briscoe suck his teeth, further displaying his jealousy.

"I don't know who got her, but I got a feeling that when we find Paris' killer, we're gonna either find Beautii or that person will know where she is. All of this shit is connected."

Tiff didn't have to tell me what I already knew. We had a lot going on, but I never thought shit would hit home and reach my child. There was so much I wanted to ask my mother about how this whole shit went down, but I knew I wouldn't be able to control how it came out. And right now wasn't the time to be pointing fingers.

"Paris is dead?" my mama asked, turning to Mo with her hand covering her mouth. "I'm so sorry, Morae." Walking over to Mo, she pulled her in for a tight hug. "When did this happen? How did this happen? Why y'all ain't say nothing?"

"There's not much to say. We found her this morning. Dead in a motel. I don't know much of anything else other than she didn't go there willingly," Mo answered. "And if y'all don't mind, I'd rather focus on finding my niece. I'm gonna get to the bottom of what happened to P."

"This is a **we** thing now, Mo," my father interjected, "and we gon' get to the bottom of all this shit. We move as a unit. And that unit now includes Justice and Santana." He cut his eye at me when he mentioned Santana. "This clown wants 50K, cool. Hogany, give Dough your phone, so he can do what he gotta do to trace the number."

I got up and handed my phone to Dough as requested. "It's unlocked. The number on the call log after Mo is the one dude called from."

"Okay," Dough replied. "If he say he want 50K, he gotta be desperate. He'll be calling back soon — if I don't pull something before then."

"Do your best, Dough," my father emphasized. "Mahogany, grab the fifty from your safe, and I'll replace it later. When you get the call with a location, we'll all be with you."

That sounded like the best idea to me. Getting up, I made my way to the den where my safe was located. Both Tiffany and Morae followed behind me.

"What you need us to do in the meantime, Hogany?" Tiff asked.

"Need you on arsenal. Gather up all the firepower you feel we need."

"On it. You wanna meet back here?"

"Yeah. We can meet back here in a couple hours. If I get the call before then, I'll let y'all know."

"Cool. Look, I want y'all to know that it's not over until we say it's over. And I'm riding with y'all through the gates of hell if that's what it takes cause I know we coming out on the other side of this."

Mo and I nodded. I proceeded to remove the portrait of Beautii as a baby from my wall, exposing one of the two safes I had in my home for emergencies. Typing in the code to get access, it opened to neatly stacked $100 bills. This particular safe held $200,000. It was all clean money, directly from my club.

"Hand me that duffle bag on the shelf please, Mo."

Tossing the 50K in the MCM duffle she gave me, I covered the safe back up and turned to Mo. Hurt was written all over her face, down to her posture. My girl had just lost her person, and here she was, standing ten toes down for me in my time of need. This was what true sisterhood was about, being there for each other, and we had that shit down to a science.

"Mo..." I went to speak, and she shook her head.

"I already know. Don't tell me what we gonna do, Hogany. Let's just do it."

"Heard." Leaving the den, we returned to the living room. I placed the duffle bag on the coffee table and walked over to Justice.

"Do you want me to drop you back off home?"

"If I wanted to be home, I would've brought my own car. I'm here to help. This is the only time I'll ever allow you to use me, so use me wisely."

I stared at him for several moments. While it may have seemed that I was staring at him in admiration, I was really trying to figure out if we were making the right decision by bringing him into the fold. Sure, his background showed that he was solid, and the way he handled the ransom call showed his ability to remain calm in tense situations, but this was my daughter's life hanging in the balance. I couldn't go into this thing second guessing anyone.

"You think out loud," he said, pulling my attention. "You don't have to trust me. My actions will speak for themselves." He grabbed my hand and rubbed it soothingly. "Let's find your baby girl."

"Yo, Hogany, let me talk to you for a minute," Briscoe called out to me.

"Go head and handle that," Justice encouraged. "I'ma see how I can help Dough trace that number."

"Thank you. And for what happened earlier..."

"Small thing to a giant. We'll talk about it some other time."

Nodding, I turned my attention to Briscoe, whose jaw was tight as he watched our interaction. I nodded for him to follow me as I walked past. Guiding him into the kitchen and out of earshot of everyone, I waited for him to speak.

"How long you known that nigga out there?"

"Not long, Briscoe. Our parents have history though. I figured you'd wanna talk about Beautii, not Justice."

"I wanna talk about anybody that just popped up outta nowhere over the last week or so. Your long-lost brother included and his girl. All these new guests could have a hand in our daughter's disappearance. I'm looking at everybody sideways right now."

"Briscoe, real shit, if your conversation doesn't consist of anything positive, like a solution, then please don't talk to me until we get our daughter back. This is a lot, and I don't need your bullshit right now." I felt the tears stinging my eyes, but I did not want to cry in front of him, especially when he was in rare form.

"You right. I'm buggin'." He spoke in a defeated tone. "This shit got my head fucked up, Hogany. Somebody did the unthinkable and now look at us. We been walking round this bitch thinking we untouchable, and they hit us in the worst way."

I felt the weight of his words. It was the most vulnerable I'd ever seen Briscoe. And despite his recent absence and the way he showed up today, I knew he loved our daughter and would do whatever necessary for her. I didn't procreate with a man who just didn't give a fuck. Feeling the need to call a truce, I spoke up.

"We can't move effectively if we beefin', Bryon." Calling him by his government name usually got his attention, and this time was no different. "Beautii needs both of her parents on one accord."

"You right. And we getting her back. I don't give a fuck who we gotta step on."

"That's the energy I need." I held out my hand for him to shake, and he pulled me in for a hug.

"I love y'all, Hogany." He spoke into my ear. "I'm dyin' bout my family."

"Hol' up." I pushed him back slightly. "Ain't nobody dyin'. If you wanna make a declaration, declare that we gon' go out here and tear shit up to get our child back. I'm not losing nobody else."

I briefly thought about Paris, a beautiful life snuffed out for no damn reason. I planned to cover whatever funeral expenses Mo allowed me to once we got around to it. She wasn't just an employee. She was family.

"That's for shit sure. Let me make some calls and put my people in position. As soon as your phone rings, I need to be the first to know."

"I got you. Listen, I don't need too many people on this, Briscoe. Only your most trusted."

"Copy."

He left the kitchen, and my head dropped. While anger filled me, fear also engulfed my body. I had no doubt in my mind that we'd bring Beautii home. The condition of her mental when she returned scared me. I didn't know that trauma firsthand, but I'd seen it inflicted on others. I didn't want my baby scarred. The hum of the refrigerator was the only thing that could be heard in the kitchen to combat my thoughts before I heard footsteps. They were strong and deliberate, alerting me to my father's presence before he could round the corner.

"Pick your head up, Mahogany," he said, his voice thick with authority.

My father stood at 6'2" with a medium build. His skin tone matched mine, and he had dark brown eyes that were intimidating yet soft when they needed to be. Lifting my head, I glanced over at him. I wanted nothing more than to collapse in his arms like a child, but he wouldn't allow it, not because he couldn't deal with the emotion but because he knew his child. My father knew that me falling apart would only hinder the search for Beautii. So, without him having to talk me into it, I straightened my posture.

"We don't have the luxury of falling apart now. I need your head on straight and at one hundred percent."

I nodded at the raw authority in his voice that sliced through my fear. "Anything on the trace?"

"Not yet. Dough is still working on it."

"Okay. I hope she can forgive me when we get her back."

"This isn't your fault. Unfortunately for us, it's part of the game."

I scoffed. "Yeah, well, unfortunately for them, they had the right idea, wrong bitch."

Walking around him, I headed back out to the living room. The waiting game was killing me, but as soon as the call came through, I was on go.

Chapter Seven

COOLIE

It hadn't been a full twenty-four hours, and I was already out of retirement and back on some deadly shit. Somebody had crossed a line that no man had dared to since I stepped foot in this game, violating my family in the worst way. My head was still reeling from how shit went down. And for the first time in over twenty years, my wife had me second guessing her moves. The safety of my family was top priority.

I made sure to drill into both Antoinette's and Mahogany's heads to triple check everything to ensure their safety. So, how someone was able to get into my house and snatch my granddaughter while Nette slept soundly had me seeing red. My plan to surprise the family with my early release had quickly turned into me prepping them for war. Watching my daughter on the verge of a breakdown put me in a headspace where I wanted to say fuck waiting on the call and just go out and get to gunning down the enemies each person had mentioned, but I didn't move on emotion. Being calculated had gotten me this far and remaining that way would ensure my granddaughter's safe return.

I hadn't mentioned it, but I had a feeling that I knew who was responsible for this. I didn't plan on sharing the information with Hogany until I was absolutely sure. Knowing my daughter, she would move as soon as she got a name, and I couldn't have that.

"What's the word, Dough?" I questioned my right hand.

"Nothing on the trace unfortunately. Which tells me that whoever the player is, they know what they doing. At the same time, they've never made a move on this scale. Not asking for no 50K, they haven't."

Nodding, I stroked my goatee. "Aight. Need you to ride with me. I'm gonna drop Antoinette back at the house. Follow me."

"Cool. I'll have Tionne sit with her. Maybe they can keep each other calm."

"Hey," I called out to Hogany, who stood off to the side, talking to Justice. "I'm gonna take Mommy home, and then I got a move to make with Dough."

She cocked an eyebrow, likely trying to figure out my plan without having to ask me. "I know you know something, and you're not telling me, Daddy. But I'll let you do what you do best. Just bring her home if you get to her before me."

"Let me know as soon as that phone rings." Kissing her forehead, I nodded at Justice. "Keep ya phone nearby."

Gathering Antoinette and Tionne, we passed Tiffany and Morae on our way out. Feeling like I needed to say something to Mo, I doubled back.

"Hey, Killa."

She looked up from her phone, mustering up a small smile.

"You know we gon' make these niggas pay, right?"

"In the worst way."

"So long as you know." I kissed her forehead and headed outside. "I'll drive," I said to Antoinette, who stood on the driver's side of the car. Without questioning my reasoning for wanting to drive, she walked around and slid into the passenger seat.

"Is there a reason I'm going home if we need to be on standby for the call?" Nette asked as we drove.

We didn't lie to each other, and I didn't plan on starting now. It was clear that she had overheard my conversation with Dough. "As soon as she gets the call, we'll know. Right now, I need you home while I make this move."

"What you going to do, Coolie? You just came home; I don't need you going back. Whatever you have planned, you need to clue me in, so we're on the same page."

"Going back to prison is the last thing on my mind when my grandbaby is missing."

I could feel her eyes on me, but I kept my focus dead locked on the road. Antoinette and I were in sync, and sometimes, she knew my thoughts before I could express them. She continued to stare for a few seconds before speaking.

"Curtis, do you know who has Beautii?" she asked straight up.

I slowed down and came to a full stop at a red light before answering her. "I don't know for sure, which is why I didn't mention it to Mahogany. But I'm damn sure about to go and find out."

"Who do you think it is?"

"You remember when Tiff was shot?"

"How could I forget? That shit had us all on edge, not knowing if she was going to make it or not. But I thought Dough took care of it?"

"Yeah, he did. But everybody has family, Nette. From what I hear, he has an older brother that's been talking about making a move on some get back shit. And if that's the case, I wanna rule him out by deading the possibility."

Confusion was written all over her face, but I had no time to paint a clearer picture for her. My silence indicated that, so she didn't pry further and remained quiet for the remainder of the drive. Pulling into my driveway, I turned the car off and turned to her.

"You know that was some amateur shit you pulled last night, right?" I asked, referring to her not ensuring that the back door to our house was locked and the alarm was activated before she went to sleep.

She went to hang her head but lifted it before her chin could hit her chest. "I'll never forgive myself for being so careless. I had a couple glasses of wine after dinner, just to wind down for the night and wait on your call and ended up falling asleep. I checked on Beautii beforehand, and she was up, watching TV. I can't even bring myself to tell Mahogany that shit. It sounds crazy even saying it out loud."

When I got locked up, Nette had expressed that she wasn't comfortable with having security around the house when I wasn't around as she didn't trust anyone outside of Dough. She begged for the state-of-the-art alarm system that we had installed under the pretense that she'd use it. The one time she didn't cost us.

"Tionne is gonna be here with you, and my people won't be too far."

Getting out of the car, I walked around to her side and opened her door. Ushering her inside, I headed straight to the basement. Strapping up, I loaded my guns with an extended clip. Niggas needed to know how I was coming off top, and I wasn't fucking around. Nette entered the basement just as I loaded the last clip into my FN.

"As your wife, I've learned to stand down, but this is my granddaughter too, so I must say something. Whatever moves you make, understand that it affects us all. I cannot lose you again."

"You know who you married, so you already know I'ma be good. I'll call you in a few. I love you." Kissing her lips for the first time since I'd been home, I headed back out.

On my way outside, I ran into Tionne as she came in.

"T…"

"Dough already filled me in. We good here. Find the princess."

"Preciate you."

Dough stood outside his car, on the phone, waiting for me.

"Where we headed?" he asked, hopping in on the passenger side.

I gave him the short version of my theory of who I thought could have Beautii, and he was down to ride just like I knew he'd be. It didn't matter that we were riding out on a thought alone. If it made sense to me, it made sense to Dough. Sitting back in his seat, he gestured for me to pull off. Typing the address into the GPS that I had for some nigga named Black, we drove into the city.

I took in the city streets as we drove, thinking about how we'd reached this point. Although I'd put Mahogany in the head seat at The Table, I was still responsible for the infrastructure. I had to make this shit right.

"So, break this shit down to me, Cool. I know I killed the nigga who shot at the girls and put Tiff in the hospital. I got the nigga hand in a jar in my basement to prove it. Where this Black character come from?"

"He's been locked up the last ten years. Just came home a couple days after you killed the brother. You know we find out shit behind the wall before it hits the streets. Hogany done made a name for herself. Somebody done put two and two together and named her as the shooter."

Pulling onto the street Black trapped on, I parked directly in front of the building, not giving a fuck who saw me. Every city block was operated under The Table, and while a lot of these new young niggas knew my name, seeing my face would be a first for some, Black included. I was prepared for the tough talk.

"Cool, you know I don't do the young nigga crowd at all. If one of these niggas so much as nod they head wrong, I'm taking it the fuck off," Dough forewarned, clicking the safety off his P365.

"Good to know that we remain on the same page after all these years." I had murder on my mind, so if anyone wanted to meet their creator before he called them, I had no issue with sending them to glory.

Stepping out of the car with my FN at my side, I pushed forward. Inside the lobby, there were a few young dudes gathered. All eyes shifted, and the atmosphere changed.

"What's good? Y'all need something?" one of the guys questioned, mugging us.

"Yeah," I responded to the spokesperson with the FN raised in his direction. "As a matter of fact, we do."

"Move an inch and I'ma paint these walls a crimson red," Dough warned the rest of the posse.

"Looking for someone by the name of Black. And before you get to doing all that *you don't know who that is* type bullshit, know that I take lying as a form of disrespect. I respond to disrespect with demise so think before you answer."

He took one look at his people, and they engaged in a silent conversation before he spoke. "Second floor. Apartment 2H."

"Preciate it. That went well. My next request may not but do remember what this FN can do to your frontal lobe if you don't comply. I need you to take me to the apartment."

He immediately shook his head no, and I responded by taking two steps forward so that I was directly in front of him. Tapping the gun on his forehead, I spoke. "You can easily use your brain to make the right decision, or we can use your brain matter as decoration for the mailboxes behind you. You got two seconds. One... t...”

“Aight, man,” he responded begrudgingly, cussing under his breath.

“Cool.” I turned to the remaining three. “The rest of y’all clear the lobby and find something safe to do. Make sure it doesn’t include speaking on what took place here.”

No one dared to move before Dough gave them the okay. When he nodded, they scurried out of the building.

“He’s on the second floor. I told you what apartment he’s in. Why you ain’t letting me go, man?”

“You spoke first,” I said to my new hood tour guide. “All I need you to do is knock and say your name.” I pushed him toward the door that read stairwell while holding onto the back of his hoodie.

“What? You want me to say my name? Do you know who Black is? That nigga is crazy as fuck!”

“Oh, word?” I responded as if I gave a fuck. “Well, my name is Coolie, and I’m insane.”

Halting his steps, he craned his neck. “Coolie? Ahhh, hell naw!”

I could hear Dough chuckle behind me, and if the matter at hand wasn’t so urgent, I would’ve laughed too. His reaction let me know that he knew who he was dealing with.

“Coolie, man, I don’t want no static.”

“Good to know. Keep walking.”

Making it up the second flight of steps, we reached apartment 2H. Looking back once more, the kid shook his head and knocked.

“Who is it?”

“It’s Tee. Black there?”

I could hear the locks twisting before the door opened. Dough wasted no time rushing the person on the other side, causing them to fall back, landing on the floor with a loud thud. Before he had a chance to recover, I stood over him with my gun pointed at his head.

“Where the fuck is Black?” I asked the scrawny, fair skinned man whose eyes were wide like he was fresh off some kind of high.

“Bl... Black?” he questioned, playing dumb.

Raising my foot, I brought it down on his ankle hard enough to hear it crack. He howled out like I knew he would, causing a figure to come rushing to the front of the apartment.

"What the fuck?" I heard and quickly turned my head just in time to see the person try to retreat to where they came from, only to be stopped by a left hook from Dough that knocked him into the wall.

Grabbing the man by his shirt, Dough held him up against the wall.

"Black?" I questioned my tour guide, who looked like he wanted to disappear.

He didn't give a verbal yes, but I caught the subtle head nod.

"Black, I'ma make this easy on you. Tell me where my grand-daughter is, so I can be on my way, and you can take ya man here to the hospital to get this ankle checked out."

"Ya granddaughter? I don't know shit about your granddaughter. Nigga, I don't even know you," he managed to get out with his face smashed up against the wall.

"You sure?"

"Hell yeah!"

"Aight. Dough, check the house."

Pushing Black's face against the wall, Dough went to conduct his search.

"It's like that, Tee? You brought these niggas up here to my shit? Wait till they leave," he threatened the kid, not knowing that he wouldn't be alive to make good on the threat.

"Somebody gotta get me to a hospital, man. My fuckin' ankle broke," the scrawny dude cried out from the floor.

"Sit down, Black," I instructed.

"Fuck no. Y'all niggas need to get out of my shit!" he barked, wanting me to think he was unfazed by the gun pointed at him.

Needing to kill that tough guy shit, I let a shot off, hitting his leg. That got him to sit down involuntarily.

"Ahh, what the fuck, man?!" he screamed, holding onto his leg.

Dough walked back out, shaking his head, letting me know that he hadn't located Beautii.

"I told you, man. You got the wrong people," Black reiterated.

Looking into his eyes, I believed him. Unfortunately, like his brother, he had to pay for just his thoughts of bringing harm to my daughter. Raising the FN, I put a bullet between his eyes and sent another through scrawny dude's chest.

Turning to the kid, I could see the fear written all over his face.

"What did you see here, Tee?"

"Nothing." He answered with no hesitation.

"Good. Within the last twenty-four hours, have you seen Black walk in or out of this building with a kid?"

"No."

"Okay. You're free to go."

"Huh?" he questioned, confused. "You're letting me go?"

"Is there a reason I shouldn't?" I countered.

"N-no."

"You sure?"

"I swear."

"Okay. You can be on your way."

He looked back-and-forth between me and Dough then at the two bodies before turning and making his way to the front door.

"Preciate your help, Tee," I said to his back.

He kept moving, and I waited until he closed the door before turning to Dough. "Call it in to Dudas."

"On it. You sure about letting the kid go?"

"Yeah. He ain't gon' talk. The fact that I let him go is fucking his head up. He gon' be too busy worrying about me coming back to take him out. We still don't have shit, Dough. I need to see my grandbaby face."

"We gon' get something," he assured me.

Time was of the essence, and with the Black character being a dead end, we were back to waiting on the phone call.

Chapter Eight

RENEE

I watched Santana pull off from the lobby in the hotel and was glad he didn't come inside when he dropped us off. I was liable to swing on his ass at any moment. I knew it wouldn't have gone over well if I did, but I was pissed the fuck off. And at this point, it felt like he was saying fuck me and our daughter since he linked up with his "family". I was over this Mahogany bitch and her bullshit. Her putting her hands on me was the last straw. There was a time where Santana would stomp a bitch out behind me, but he didn't even rush her or nothing when she had her hands around my neck. I was embarrassed but hurt above everything.

"You okay, Ma?" Asia asked as we entered the room.

"Yeah. I'm fine. You hungry?" Dropping my bag on the small table in the room, I sat down, and Asia sat across from me.

"No. I had some snacks back at Aunty Mahogany house."

Hearing my daughter refer to that deranged bitch as aunty irked me. "That ain't yo' aunt. That's yo daddy sister."

"Which makes her my aunt, Ma," she stated matter factly in that condescending tone of her father's that I hated.

"Yeah, but..." I caught myself before I went in. As close as Asia and

47

her father were, I knew anything I said to her was like telling him. I loved their bond, but that was the one thing I hated. "Nevermind."

"I hope they find Beautii soon. I can't believe somebody took her, Ma. That could've been me."

"No the hell it couldn't. Unlike her mother, I'm not letting you out my sight for too long." Her face frowned up like she was offended by what I said. Ignoring it, I stood. "I'm gonna go take a shower." I absent-mindedly rubbed my neck, stopping when she looked at it. "If you get hungry while I'm in there, just order room service. If your dad calls, bring me the phone." I planned to deny his call as soon as it came in. I didn't have shit to say to him.

"Okay."

Heading to the bathroom, I stripped out of my clothes. Turning the shower on, I made it as hot as I could stand it and stepped inside. As the water hit my body, I sighed. This whole being in New York thing was not working out the way I envisioned. While I was all for supporting my man and his rise to the top and takeover, each day that passed, it seemed like Santana was losing sight of the plan — that or he had abandoned it altogether and had neglected to tell me.

That was so like Santana too. Yeah, I knew my nigga loved me, but he also had a selfish way about him. I was sure he got that shit from his mean ass father. The way he reacted today told me everything I needed to know. Rather than keeping to the task at hand, he wanted to be accepted. And that was cool because I wanted him to have a relationship with his people — but not at the expense of me being uncomfortable.

"Ma," I heard Asia call out before entering the bathroom.

"Yeah?"

"Your phone. You have a missed call."

"Okay, was it Daddy?"

"No. Somebody named Rita."

Quickly snatching the shower curtain back, my eyes widened, and my heart thumped. "Did you answer?"

"No. I said you had a missed call, Ma."

"Oh, right." I let out a nervous giggle. "You can put it on the counter. I'm getting out now. Thanks, baby."

"No problem."

I watched as she set the phone down before leaving the bathroom. Hopping out of the shower, still wet, I carefully tiptoed over to the door and locked it. Grabbing a towel from the rack, I wrapped it around my body and picked the phone up to dial the number back. As it rang, I turned on the sink in an effort to drown out my conversation.

"Hello," I whispered once the call connected after a few rings.

"Fuck is you whispering for?"

"Cause I'm not alone, Razor." Asia wasn't a nosey child but a child nonetheless. I had to be cautious.

"Santana around?"

"No. It's just me and Asia. What's wrong? Why you sound like that?"

"You at the hotel?"

"Yeah. Just got out the shower. Hold on, I'm gonna FaceTime you," I replied with a sneaky smile.

"Nah. Not right now." He stopped me, causing my smile to drop. "I need you to meet me."

"Okay, when? I can get an Uber now. Send me your location."

"I'ma send it, but I need you to meet me there at 4:30."

"Why 4:30? Why can't I just come now?"

"What the fuck I just say, Renee?"

Sucking my teeth, I sighed. "Alright, Razor. I'll be there at 4:30."

I was making plans and didn't have the slightest clue as to what I was gonna do with Asia.

"Aight. Don't flake on me, Renee. I really need you. This dick need you the most."

I squeezed my legs together, thinking about the heights his dick took me to every time we fucked. There was no denying Santana's stroke game, but he didn't have shit on Razor.

"I'll be there."

"Cool. Sending you the information now."

Hanging up, I got dressed and lounged around the hotel for a few hours with Asia. I made sure to let her order all the room service her little heart desired. When the time rolled around for me to meet up with Razor, I texted him that I would see him in a few and that I couldn't stay long seeing as there was no one to look after her while I was gone.

He didn't respond, and that was fine by me so long as he didn't change his mind about me coming.

"Hey, boo," I said to Asia, who was glued to her phone. "I need to run out for a few, but I won't be gone long. You okay with being here by yourself?"

I'd let her stay home alone plenty of times, but I didn't know how comfortable she'd feel at a hotel in a different city. I held my breath, awaiting her response. I needed a tune up, so I silently hoped that my girl would take one for the team and hold it down.

Looking up from her phone, she gave me questioning eyes. "Where you going?"

I had no immediate response to her question but knew I had to come up with something to tell her. "Out for a minute, Asia. I'll be back. Are you okay with being here?"

Checking my watch, the time read 3:40, and according to my Uber app, my driver would be arriving in three minutes.

"Okay. I'll be fine."

"You sure?"

"I'm twelve, Ma. I'm sure."

"Well, alright. Call me if you need anything. Don't call your dad. He needs to focus on finding Beautii." I threw the last part in there as a precautionary measure.

"Okay."

Kissing her forehead, I grabbed my purse and made my way out the door. After the morning I had, I knew the hurting Razor put on my pussy would make me feel a lot better.

WHEN I ARRIVED AT THE ADDRESS RAZOR HAD GIVEN ME, I had to double check to make sure it was right. The neighborhood was quiet, and single family homes lined the block. It didn't seem like a place he would be, but I went with it.

"Thank you," I said to the Uber driver as I exited the car.

Checking my phone, I sent a text to Asia to make sure she was good. She responded back immediately that I hadn't been gone long enough to be checking in so soon. I smiled and shook my head at my grown little lady. Placing the phone on vibrate, I tucked it in my bag. Walking up to the door of the house, I knocked, and Razor answered seconds later.

"Come in," he said, pulling me inside without so much as a hello.

I watched as he scanned outside before closing the door behind me.

"I see we're being rude today."

"Nah. Just making sure you weren't followed. Come on."

I walked behind him and found myself looking around, wondering whose house he had me in. The place had a homely feel, but something felt off.

"It's an Airbnb," he informed me before I could ask.

He guided me to the living room where I took a seat on the couch, removing my coat. Sitting next to me, he grabbed at my thigh and squeezed. The slight touch of his hand made my pussy moist. You would think I was sex deprived by the throbbing between my legs. And that wasn't the case, seeing as Santana made sure to slide up in me every chance he got.

Razor had a different touch though. It was just what I was craving in the moment. Making the first move, I leaned in, kissing his neck while rubbing my hand up his thigh. Grabbing a handful of his dick through his jeans, I felt it harden in my hand. Just as I went to turn it up a notch and unbuckle his belt, he put his hand on mine, stopping me.

"What's wrong with you?" I asked, pulling my lips from his neck. "I thought you said you missed me and wanted to see me."

"I got something to show you. But before I do, I need to know that I can trust you."

"Razor, you know you can trust me."

"Nah. This shit is heavy. I need to know you really ridin' for a nigga. And if you are, I need to hear you say it. Where we bout to go, ain't no turning back the clock. So, I need to know, Renee."

"What the hell, Razor? You scaring me."

"Forget it," he said, standing and turning to walk away.

I jumped up from the couch and pulled at his arm. "Wait. Yes, I'm down for you. As much information as I've been feeding you about Santana, you gotta know I'm down. It's me and you, bae."

Nodding, he kissed my lips and grabbed my hand. "That's what I wanna hear."

Intertwining his fingers with mine, he walked me through the house and down a short hall. Stopping at a closed door, he glanced over at me. Not knowing what to expect, I squeezed his hand and flashed an uneasy smile. Twisting the doorknob, he pushed it open, and my bottom lip damn near hit the floor when I stepped inside and saw Beautii lying on the bed with her hands and feet tied and tape on her mouth.

"What the fuck, Razor?! Are you fucking crazy? Do you know who the fuck that is?" I started toward her, and he pulled me back by my shirt, out the door.

Closing it behind me, he shot me a pissed off stare. I didn't give a fuck because this was some crazy shit.

"Razor, what are you doing with that little girl? Do you know that's Mahogany's daughter? Her people are looking for her. I was literally just at a meeting her family was having, trying to get her back. They got all hands on deck. And when I say all hands, I mean every last one of them crazy motherfuckas. I would have still been there now if that crazy bitch, Mahogany, didn't try to choke me out. Razor, what the hell? Say somethin'." I had been rambling so much, I needed to catch my breath.

"I'll speak as soon as you shut the fuck up. Come on." He grabbed my hand again, this time pulling me back to the living room — and not in a loving manner. "You doing all that damn talking right outside the room where she can hear you. This is the big payday I've been looking for. And if you help me with this, there's something in it for you too. I've been working with a contact, one that has been guiding me in the right direction to take all this shit over. Snatching shorty wasn't a part of the initial plan, but the slight detour will turn out to be lucrative in the end. You said you ridin', right?"

The whole time he spoke, my life literally flashed before my eyes. I knew no matter what I said, my answer would change the course of my entire life anyway. I could tell him no, leave, and go right to Mahogany and tell her I knew exactly where her daughter was. I could leave, tell Santana I found Beautii, and text him the address to get her. Or I could return Beautii myself and help Razor come up with another plan to get money and take over.

The longer I thought, the dumber each plan sounded. Each plan led to my relationship being exposed, Santana leaving me, and Mahogany likely trying to kill me. Razor was currently my only ally. And quiet as it was kept, I wanted to knock Mahogany down off that high horse she'd been riding since the day I met her. The thought of making money while doing it made me inclined to help him, but I was not with hurting Beautii at all.

"If I help you with this, Razor, you have to promise we won't get caught. This Table shit is very much real. These people are nothing to play with. And the Coolie guy is home. That motherfucka is a beast on his own, and with Mahogany being spawned from him, this plan has to be airtight."

"It's tighter than that pussy, baby. Ain't no way we can lose. I promise you that. This her only kid, so she's going to make sure we get the bread I asked for. If it's one thing them motherfuckas got, it's money. We just gotta move accordingly, and if we do this shit right, we ain't ever gon' get caught. You just gotta trust me, baby."

"I trust you," I spoke softly.

Wrapping his arms around my waist, he pulled me into him and kissed my lips. The kiss was so passionate that I felt my knees buckle.

"You got my dick so hard," he whispered. "You know yo' loyalty turns me on."

Picking me up, he carried me two rooms down from where Beautii was. Entering the bedroom, he laid me down gently on the bed. I watched as he pulled his shirt over his head and stripped out of his jeans. Following suit, I undressed, leaving only my thong on. I enjoyed watching him peel them off me with his teeth.

"I missed you so much," I expressed, hitching in a breath when he licked along my waistline, pulling at my thong with his teeth.

Sliding them off, he spread my legs wide. Kneeling so that he was eye level with my pussy, he placed a gentle kiss on it. A moan escaped my lips as he licked up and down my slit. Knowing just what to do, he slurped my clit into his mouth and sucked on it. It was only the beginning, and I was squirming already. Razor was a pussy eating fool and didn't stop feasting on me until I'd cum twice.

The high was never ending as he climbed on top of me and slid his thick dick inside my wet box.

"Shiiidd," he crooned. "It's always tight for me, baby. I love this pussy."

Loving the way he complimented my tight walls, I wrapped my legs around him, pulling him in deeper. It was important for me to have him just as gone over me as I was over him. Grinding my hips so that I met each thrust, I felt myself on the brink of release again. Wanting him to cum with me, I did a kegel that made him bite his lip and sink his teeth into my neck.

"Ughh, I'm cummin', Daddy!" I shrieked, and he grunted, leaving his seeds inside of me.

"Hurry up... and go pee," he let out breathlessly while rolling over on the side of me. "Bathroom is across the hall."

Picking up my clothes from the floor, I went to do as instructed, not the least bit offended. I had love for Razor, but I didn't wanna bear his children. That would be going too far. After flushing his potential children down the toilet, I redressed myself. As I went to leave the bathroom, I could hear Beautii crying. The mother in me couldn't just ignore it, so I went over to the room she was being held in.

Slowly opening the door, I entered the room to find her balled up in a fetal position with her back facing the wall.

"Beautii," I called out her name, but she didn't turn around. "Beautii," I called out again, this time closer to the bed.

She turned with a scowl on her face, one that I'd seen before.

"Hey, have you eaten?"

She stared blankly at me, and I stepped forward to remove the tape from her lips.

"Food, no. Snacks, yes. I don't wanna eat. I wanna go home. Did my mom send you?"

"Ummm, no," I responded, feeling like shit as the tears continued to fall down her cheeks.

"Why am I here? Do you know that man? Why are you here? Can you call my mom?"

She asked all the right questions to which I had all the wrong answers. I was just as foul as Razor's ass. "I can't call your mom right now, Beautii. But I can get you something to eat. I can assure you that Ra…" I caught myself before I blurted out Razor's name. "I can assure you that that man isn't going to hurt you."

"He snatched me from my grandmother's house, threw me in the trunk, and threatened to send me to my mom in pieces if I screamed. And you ain't no better than him, I see. I'm not hungry. I want to go home."

Though the tears were still present, there was strength in her tone. She was her mother's child for sure.

"I'm sorry. I have to put this tape back over your mouth." Gently covering her mouth, I walked out as quietly as I'd come in. Closing the door behind myself, I ran into Razor.

"Dammit, Razor. Why you here ear hustling?"

"Why you in there talkin' to her without telling me?"

Sucking my teeth, I walked past him toward the front of the house like it was mine. "She was crying. I couldn't just ignore her." Heading into the kitchen, I checked the cabinets and fridge to see if there was anything I could whip up. "Damn, you don't have anything for her to eat?"

"This an Airbnb, Renee. You know damn well they don't provide food."

"Well, I'm sure she's hungry. Have you heard from your contact yet?"

"Nah, I should be getting a call any minute now though."

"Okay. Hopefully, that's sooner than later. We gotta feed her. What good is your plan if she dies of starvation?"

"The fuck is you talkin' bout starvation? You actin' like I've had her for week. And she ate a bag of chips earlier."

"Boy, either order something to eat or give me your keys, so I can go get something. It's almost five thirty in the evening, and all that little girl had to eat was some damn chips? That's so trifling."

Shrugging his shoulders, he reached into his pocket and tossed me his keys. Letting him know that I'd be back in a few, I hopped in the car and used the GPS to guide me to the nearest grocery store. I knew I wouldn't be able to prepare her a full meal, but I could throw something together real quick that would hold her over.

MAKING IT TO A FINE FARE, I SCANNED THE AISLES, grabbing ingredients to make sandwiches. As I walked through the supermarket, my phone rang in my purse. Taking it out, seeing Santana's name pop up on the screen, my stomach felt queasy. I didn't think he'd call before I made it back to the hotel.

"**Hello?**" I answered in an even tone, not wanting to let on to my nervousness.

"**Where the fuck you at?! I just came back to the hotel, and you got our kid here by herself.**"

"**I'm at the store.**"

"**The store? Did your silly ass forget we out here in the middle of a damn war?!**" he barked.

"**I don't have nothing to do with no damn war. Hell, neither do you but you insist on inserting yo'self into the bullshit, which is crazy to me. And the fact you doin' this shit for a bitch that don't even like you is even crazier.**" I bucked back at him.

"**That bitch is my sister, which makes the missing little girl my niece. So, I have everything to do with this. And as a mother, you knowing that there's a fucking child out there missing and leaving yo' own child at a hotel by herself is crazy as fuck. Not to mention irresponsible. The fuck is wrong witchu? Where yo' head at, man?**"

"**Santana, I...**"

"**Don't even answer that. Get back here and get back here now, Renee. I have moves to make.**"

Sucking my teeth, I rolled my eyes. "**I'll be there within the hour.**"

"**Make it sooner.**"

Ending the call without a response, I pushed my cart up to the register to check out. Paying with the cash I had on me, I headed back to the house. When I returned, Razor opened the door with his phone to his ear. From what I could catch of the conversation without being too nosey, it sounded like he was on the phone with his contact. I could hear him confirming a drop point for Mahogany to deliver the money.

Busying myself with making a turkey and cheese sandwich for Beautii, I continued to listen.

"Stop being nosey and go take the kid the food," he said, catching me slippin' as he ended the call. "As a matter of fact, I'll give it to her."

"I wasn't even paying attention to you," I countered, placing the sandwich on a plate and pouring her a cup of juice. "I gotta go anyway. Santana called while I was at the supermarket. I gotta get Asia."

"Aight. I need yo' ears open and yo' mouth closed on this one."

"What you mean my mouth closed?"

"Just what I said. I need you to play it cool. Don't go giving no unnecessary problems. Just sit back and be observant, aight?"

"Mmmhmm. I hear you." Taking out my phone, I ordered another Uber back to the hotel.

Razor walked up on me and kissed my forehead. "Thanks for the way you came through today and being solid."

"Told you I got you."

After a thirteen-minute wait for the Uber, I was on my way back to the hotel. The whole way back, I prepared for all the questions that Santana would probably ask about my absence. I knew my tale of running out to the store and leaving Asia behind didn't go over well with him, so I made sure to take a bag of snacks that I'd picked up. When I arrived at the hotel room, he was standing at the window.

"I'm back," I announced. "Why you lookin' out the window?"

"I'm tryna see if I can see where you lost your rabbit ass mind," he replied, turning to me with a scowl on his face.

"Oh, God. Santana, please." I sat the bag down and started to walk back to our room but didn't get far before he snatched me back by my arm.

"Are you fuckin' cool? Cause you actin' like you don't understand what's going on. Shit is critical right now. We don't know who's behind this shit. For all I know, they could be gunnin' for me too. Which makes you and Asia a target. You can't move how you wanna move. You gotta sit the fuck still until I give you further instruction. And if you got a problem with doing that, you need to pack both of y'all up now, so we can go to my mama house."

"I already told you we're not going there." I recoiled.

"It's either that or you stay in this room, but those are your only two options."

"Or we can just go back to the West Coast." At this point, I felt like fuck his plan and fuck the family too.

"Aight." Walking away from me, he made his way out the door.

Right then, I felt like he chose his side, so I had to do what I felt was best for me and mine.

Chapter Nine

MORAE

"*I've been waiting to taste you all night,*" *I whispered to Paris, whose legs were spread wide, playing with her pink pearl.*

Her pussy lips glistened, as her juices seeped out of her and down her fingers. Peeling out of my bodysuit, my titties sprang free, and she smiled, licking her lips. Paris always made it a point to tell me that I had the most perfect titties she'd ever seen. If she had to pick a favorite part on my body, it would be my 40Ds. Removing my panties, I climbed on the bed and lowered my pussy to her mouth in the 69 position. Paris kept her pussy waxed while I opted for a thin layer of hair to cover my mound.

WHAP! She slapped my ass hard before sucking my clit into her mouth.

"Ooouuu," I crooned, the feeling of her tongue putting me in a state of pure bliss.

Kissing her pussy softly, I mimicked her tongue movements. She moaned her satisfaction, making my clit swell. It was always a pleasurable experience eating Paris' pussy. We were always willing to take each other on a wild ride in the name of a beautiful orgasm.

"Ssssss, Moooo!" She cried out once I slipped my finger in her ass while simultaneously circling my tongue around her clit.

It didn't take long for the floodgates to open, and I watched in delight aa she squirted. Not breaking my focus, I rotated my hips, feeding her my fat cat. I'd had my fair share of dick, but there was nothing like a woman's touch when it came to pussy eating.

"Shiidd, P, I'm cummin'," I announced, grinding on her face until I came in her mouth.

With our first orgasm out of the way, we slithered our bodies into our favorite position. Something about the feeling of her pussy pressed against mine in the scissoring position always took me over the edge.

"I love you so much, Morae," P expressed, intertwining her hand with mine.

"I love you too, P."

"Mo, Mo!" Tiff yelled out my name, pulling me from the thoughts of the last intimate moment I shared with Paris. "You good?"

I nodded, staring down at her side of the bed. Tears welled up in my eyes, blurring my vision. The twinge in my heart caused an aching that I wanted so badly to suppress under the circumstances. But the reality of Paris' loss felt heavier here than it did back at the hotel. It was in this room that she shared her fears with me. This room was where we talked about our five-year plan and what life would look like for us. There was a quiet now, a silence that stretched across the room that was once filled with her laughter.

"I'm not good, Tiff," I admitted. "But I will be."

"Mo, take a minute. I'll be out front, packing everything up."

"I can't."

"You have to. I'll be right out front, sis. I love you." She hugged me from behind and walked out of the room.

I sat on the edge of the bed and didn't bother wiping the tears that fell. My world had been severed within the last few hours. And the saddest thing was that I didn't get a chance to make shit right with Paris. I'd let my stubbornness drive my emotions. The memories we shared were sure to be a blessing and a curse, a tether to her and a constant reminder that she wasn't here to make new ones with me. Closing my eyes tightly, I asked God to forgive any transgressions and grant safe passage into his arms.

I couldn't change what happened but a life for my loss would even the score. Wiping my face, I stood and walked into the bathroom to get myself together. Cleaning my face, I regained my composure and headed out to the living room. Feeling my phone vibrate in my back pocket, I hoped that it wasn't Paris' aunt calling again. I pulled it out to check, and seeing my father's name on the caller ID, I felt the same hesitance to answer but knew I had to.

"Hello."

"I only called to let you know I'm here. Whatever you need, your dad got you."

"You know?"

"Yeah. Dudas called and told me to call you."

I nodded at my brother fully stepping into his big brother role. He knew me well enough to know that I wouldn't be able to accept anything he had to say in the moment, so he sent my dad.

"Thank you, Daddy. I don't need anything right now. Beautii is missing and finding her is the main focus right now."

"You shittin' me. Missing? What the fuck is going on?"

"Your guess is as good as mine." I continued toward the living room and found Tiff leaned over the couch, holding her chest. **"Dad, let me hit you back."**

"Alright. Let me know if there's any way I can help at all. I'm gonna keep Monk Man here at the house until shit dies down."

"Okay. I love you, Dad."

"Love you too."

I ended the call, and Tiff stood up straight, anguish written all over her face.

"Tiff, you good?"

"Yeah, I'm good."

"You lyin'. I know you, Tiffany. What's wrong?"

"My chest hurts," she revealed. Since it didn't take much prying to get her to admit it, I knew she was in pain. "It started before I left the house this morning. And after we left Paris, it got worse. I just been pushing through and tryna block out the pain. I know how y'all can get, and with me just getting back and all this shit going on, there's no time for slowing down." She winced and sat on the arm of the couch.

"Did you take your medicine this morning?"

"Nah. I need to be fully alert. The medicine makes me groggy."

She placed her hand to her chest, and I knew the pain was getting the best of her. Here she was, pushing herself through pain in silence to be there for the crew. If Hogany or even her father caught wind of it, they'd have her ass on permanent time out. Not to mention my brother cuttin' up.

"Does Money know that you're not taking the medicine and thugging it out?" I asked while going into the kitchen to grab her a bottle of water. I didn't know what it would do for the pain, but it seemed like the right thing.

"No, Mo. He doesn't, and I wanna keep it that way. When he left out last night on that last minute job, I told him I was good." She grabbed the water from me and took a sip.

"I'm not gonna volunteer the information, but if he asks me, I'm telling him." She curled her lip into a scowl, and I shrugged my shoulders. "I don't care. You don't have to deal with him like I have to deal with him. For now, sit here and I'll load the bags in the car."

She reluctantly agreed and slid down onto the couch and closed her eyes. Had I not picked up on it, she would've continued in the same state, not mentioning a word to anyone. I admired Tiffany's strength, but at times, especially times like this, it could come with a cost. I couldn't have the cost be her trip to the hospital. Just as I went to place my twin AKs in the second duffle bag, my doorbell rang. Checking the peephole, I could see Dudas on the other side. I unlocked the door, and before saying anything, he pulled me into his arms.

"I'm sorry, sis," he offered empathetically.

"Thank you," I replied softly.

"I wanted to come by earlier, but I got your text and figured space was best."

"Come in," I offered. "Did you find out anything? And were you able to go by her aunt's house?"

He shook his head. "The hotel had cameras but not all of them worked. On the camera, you can see Paris clearly, but the dude she was with was able to avoid being caught on camera due to the hoodie he wore over his head when they entered. The only shots the camera picked up from him was from behind. To a normal person, they looked like another couple coming into the motel. To the trained eye, it was clear by Paris' body language that something was off. All we have is the desk clerk's description of him, which wasn't much. She basically described every nigga in New York unfortunately. I was gonna head over to her aunt's place once I left here."

"Damn, okay. I gotta call Ms. Reece. I can't let all this time pass, and she don't know nothin'. Right now, we gotta find Beautii."

"What you mean find Beautii?"

"Someone snatched her up late last night," Tiffany informed him as she sat up.

"What the hell? Did y'all report it? Let me look into it."

"Come on, Dudas. You know we ain't callin' for no police assistance on this. The moment we make this a police thing, our chances of getting Beautii back will be cut in half. The person wants 50K for her return. We're gonna pay it and get her back. We're handling it. Quiet and under the radar."

"I wouldn't call shit that got to do with an AK quiet, Mo." He pointed to the open duffle bag. "And I know Hogany ain't just gon' let this shit slide. Neither one of y'all."

"Dudas, the less you know about our movements, the better. Just know we'll have Beautii back soon. You just have our back if anything goes left. Gimmie a second. I gotta make this phone call."

Walking into the kitchen, I dialed Ms. Reece's number. My hands were shaky as I typed in each number, fighting against my emotions. Pressing the call button, the phone didn't ring once before she answered.

"Hello? Morae, honey, have you heard from her? I've been waiting for this phone to ring and so far, nothing. I don't have a good feeling. Something ain't right."

I listened to her as she spoke a truth that I hadn't confirmed yet. **"Ms. Reece, I'm so sorry. Paris was found a couple hours ago. Somebody killed her."**

"Oh, Lord, no. Lord, no."

"I'm so sorry that I didn't call sooner. I... I..." My words got caught in my throat.

"I understand, baby." She sniffled. **"I understand."**

"I'm gonna come by soon if that's okay. I have a family emergency I'm dealing with, but I'll be over there soon."

"Lord, how I'ma tell this baby his mama ain't comin' back home? What do you say to a child? Lord, give me strength."

Fresh tears fell from my eyes as I held the phone up to my ear. **"I'll be there soon,"** was all I could get out.

"Okay. Be safe out there, Morae."

"I will." Ending the call quickly, I wiped my tears. The hardest part still wasn't over. Heading back to the living room, both Tiffany and Dudas looked up at me from the couch where Dudas now sat.

"You alright?" Dudas asked.

"I have to be. We got bodies to catch."

He stared at me and Tiff for a few moments before nodding. I knew he wanted to say more, even protest our method, but there was no talking us out of the inevitable. Running his hands down his face, he spoke. "Y'all gotta let me know before y'all make a move. We gotta always remain two steps ahead of the bureau. Anything I can do on my end to ensure Beautii's safe return, I'll do it. All y'all gotta do is say the word." Turning his head to Tiff, he reached over and squeezed her leg. "You, take it easy. Can't have you in the hospital again."

She nodded with a light smile.

"I'm gonna head out," he announced, getting up and heading back to the door. "Be careful, Morae. I know The Table needs you, but so do your brothers and our father."

"I know. And I will be. You be careful too. I love you, Maurice."

"I love you too, sis."

I opened the door and watched him make his way to the elevator. As he stepped on, my phone vibrated again. This time, it was a text message from Mahogany.

Hogany: He sent a text. He's gonna call with a location in an hour. Get here as soon as y'all can.

Me: On the way.

"Mahogany texted. We gotta move, Tiff. You straight?"

She jumped up from the couch, putting her coat on. "Let's go."

The next hour would determine where we were headed. Whether we had a solid plan of action or not, the field was where you could find us.

Chapter Ten

MAHOGANY

It had been hours since I'd received another call, and I couldn't sit. My leg jumped, and I'd checked my phone so many times that I just turned the passcode option off completely. Everyone had left the house, leaving me and Justice behind. My father wanted us to operate as a team on this, but as Beautii's mother, I felt like I should've been doing more. She was out there, scared and alone, waiting on her mommy to come to her rescue. And all I could do was sit here, waiting for a bum on the other end of the phone to call back and dangle her return in my face as if she were invaluable.

The whole waiting game was going against every instinct I had as a mother. Standing abruptly, I snatched my coat up from the couch and headed to the front door. To hell with the plan. No one could feel what I felt as the woman who'd carried Beautii in my womb for nine months. My hand clenched tightly as I held onto the doorknob until I heard Justice's voice from behind me.

"Mahogany." He called my name. His voice was low, calm, and steady — the exact opposite of what I felt.

I went to speak when I felt his hand wrap around my waist. I hitched in a breath when he pulled me into him. Everything in me wanted to push him back, but my body wouldn't move.

"I can't just..." My voice cracked. "I can't just sit here, Justice. What kind of mother just sits here while someone decides her child's fate?"

Turning me to face him, he took a half step back and pointed at my chest.

"Who are you?"

"What?"

"Who are you?"

"I don't have no time for no pep talks, Justice." I waved him off.

"Good, cause I wasn't bout to give you one," he retorted. "I will tell you some real shit though. You are Mahogany fuckin' Wright. Daughter of Coolie Wright. Motherfuckas don't take from you without consequences. We getting ya lil' girl back. I know you know that, so we gotta move like that at all times."

I took in his words, nodding my agreement. The doorbell rang, interrupting the moment we shared. Checking the security cameras on my phone, I could see Briscoe standing on the other side of the door, looking just as I felt.

"No call yet?" he questioned as I let him inside.

"Not yet," I replied, closing the door behind him.

I watched as he sized Justice up with his eyes before walking farther into the house. Shaking his head, Justice gestured for me to walk ahead of him. I did to keep space between the two. As I went to ask Briscoe if he'd heard anything, my phone rang in my hand. Seeing the same number from earlier on the screen, my heartrate raced.

"It's him," I revealed, causing Briscoe to spin around and rush to my side.

"Pick up," he pushed. "And put it on speakerphone."

Connecting the call, I put it on speaker. **"Hello?"**

"You got that bread?" the man asked.

"Yes. Is my daughter good?"

"She's safe and will remain that way so long as you do your part. The moment you deviate, I'ma have to do what I gotta do. Feel me?"

I wanted to say, *yeah, bitch ass nigga*, but stern looks from both Justice and Briscoe made me change my mind. **"Yeah. I hear you."**

My blood boiled hearing this nigga threaten my kid's life. He just kept digging his grave deeper and deeper. Briscoe gestured with his hand, letting me know he wanted to speak, but I couldn't chance it. We'd tried that with Justice getting on the phone, and it was already clear he wanted to hear from me only.

"I got what you asked for. When and where can we meet?"

"I'ma text you the lo, and you need to meet me there in two hours. Not a minute sooner or a second later. Make sure you come alone. You bring anyone with you, the deal is done, and your daughter is dead. Please, for her sake, don't play with me."

"I need to see my baby. I'll follow your rules. Please let me see her. Just so I know that she's okay."

The line went silent, and my hands felt clammy. Briscoe's jaw flexed, and Justice stood back calmly. The few seconds of silence were too long for me. However, the call was still connected, so he hadn't hung up. My phone vibrated with a message that I quickly opened. It was a picture of Beautii, propped up against a white wall as if she were taking a passport picture.

"There's your proof. See you in two hours." The phone went dead, and it took everything in me not to launch it across the room.

"Ahhhh!!" I screamed out. "I'm going to torture this nigga!"

My fucking child looked helpless. I could tell she hadn't had proper sleep, and who knew if she was even being fed?

Briscoe turned away from me, void of words. My phone chimed, and another two messages came through from the number. He sent the address and reiterated that I was to go alone.

"He sent the address."

"You're not going alone," Briscoe let me know.

"Yes, I am. That nigga is desperate, and I'm not about to play with him. I'm not willing to risk that he won't really act on his word."

I texted Mo and Tiffany as I spoke. I didn't know what Briscoe was talking about. I planned on following every direction down to the letter.

"You hardheaded as hell, man. That's always been your fuckin' problem."

"Check this out," Justice intervened. "I know I'm new around these parts, but you not bout to keep barkin' on her. You making an already tense situation worse, bruh."

"Nigga, fu..." Briscoe didn't finish his sentence before Justice upped his gun on him.

"I'm the type to make an example out of niggas. I'm not with the back-and-forth."

"What the fuck y'all got going on?" I heard my dad's voice and looked past Justice to see him walking in with my mother, Dough, Aunty Tionne, and Santana.

I stepped back to let them men deal with they shit. I had to get my mind right anyway.

"Y'all better get this nigga," Briscoe said. "All that we a team shit going right out the window quick."

"I can't believe y'all in here actin' an ass during this time." My mother pointed out. Justice put his gun down without having to be asked. "Briscoe, that's your daughter out there, and you're letting your jealousy get the best of you. The last thing on your mind should be where the help is coming from so long as we have the damn help."

"Oh, yeah?" He challenged. "Well, if the first thing on your mind was ensuring my daughter's safety, we wouldn't be here now."

Before anyone knew what was happening, my father hit Briscoe with a mean left hook that sent him stumbling backward. "That was your last warning. Ain't no more passes, lil nigga."

Holding his now leaking mouth, Briscoe nodded with no rebuttal. He knew he was deadass wrong.

Grabbing a box of tissues from my coffee table, I handed it to him. "Maybe now you'll chill out."

"What happened, Mahogany?" my father questioned casually, not giving a fuck about Briscoe's snot box.

"The guy finally called and sent an address for the exchange. He wants me to come alone. Briscoe is against it, but I'm going. He specifically said alone, or Beautii is dead. There's really nothing to think about."

"That's the one thing I can agree with him on. You're not going alone."

"Daddy, the nigga didn't give me no choice. I go alone, or Beautii is dead. What are we talkin' about here?"

"I heard you the first time, and you heard me. You're not going out there uncovered. He has the upper hand right now, but we're gonna find a way to ensure Beautii's safety as well as yours. Fellas, let me talk to y'all."

My father walked out with the guys following behind him, and I shook my head.

"I hate when he does this shit," I said, plopping down on the couch with my head in my hands.

"You know how ya father can get, boo," my mother said. "It's all for the greater good though. You'll see. We gettin' my grandbaby back tonight."

"I don't know what I'ma do if we don't, Ma. I'm hanging on by a thread."

"I know, baby. I know."

An hour later, Tiff and Mo arrived, equipped with everything I'd asked for.

"I need to talk to y'all in private," I said to the two in a hushed tone. "Let's go up to my bedroom."

We separated from everyone and made our way upstairs. Once inside my room, I closed and locked the door.

"You going rogue, ain't you?" Mo said before I could get a word out.

"Nobody's listening when I'm stressing the importance of me doing this shit alone. Briscoe and my father are on the same page, and he just tried to take this nigga head off."

"I hear you, and I understand their concerns as well," Mo reasoned. "Let's just figure out a way we can make this shit happen to where we all feel good about it."

"I got it!" Tiff let out, animated. "You can meet him at the location, but we'll pull up before you. We'll all drive separate cars and spread out so that it doesn't look suspicious. We'll stay in our cars too. The moment you let us know you have her, we snatch the nigga and take it from there."

I nodded slowly, visualizing her plan in my head. "Okay. I can work with that."

"I feel like we need to pray," Mo suggested. "Feels like we need it more now than ever. I just wanna send one up for Beautii's safe return, our protection..."

"And this Glock not jammin' on me," Tiff interrupted.

I smirked and grabbed hold of both of their hands, giving them a light squeeze. Bowing our heads, Mo sent up a prayer that soothed my heart. By the time she was done, we all were crying. We hadn't been vulnerable with each other in so long, and the tears were silent admissions of how scared we really were. I wanted to use the fear of the unknown to propel us forward. I had to continue to move with confidence to let them know we had this shit — even when it didn't look like it.

Getting ourselves together, we walked back downstairs. Back in the living room, I stood in the entryway with Tiff and Mo in their places, to the left and right of me.

"Everyone, listen up real quick," I spoke, and all eyes turned in my direction. "This is the plan. We're all headed out to the destination, but I'll be riding alone. Briscoe, you'll ride with Tiff and Mo. Daddy, Mommy, and Santana will ride together. Justice, you'll be with Dough and Aunty T. We move smart and not on emotion. I'm texting the address to each of you, and I want y'all to leave out before me. Park within a block of the area. I'll call Tiff once I have Beautii, and we go from there. I'm not taking any suggestions. This is the plan." I eyed everyone in the room with my eyes landing on my father last. He nodded his understanding, and I nodded my appreciation. "Aight, strap up so we can go get our baby."

WHILE THE GPS ESTIMATED A FORTY-FIVE-MINUTE TRAVEL time to the location, I took a detour that added an additional fifteen minutes so that I arrived in the hour timeframe the man had given me. I didn't want to give him any reason to back out and take off with Beautii again. I hadn't told the family that part of the plan, and it was for the best. As I drove, I glanced at the screensaver on my phone. It was a candid picture Beautii had taken of us when we were on our way out to one of our mommy and daughter spa dates.

The bond that we shared was so tight; I had a feeling she knew I was on my way to her. That thought alone made me press on the gas a little harder, needing to get there. When the GPS confirmed that I was a minute out, my phone rang with an incoming call from my father.

"We're here. Parked around the corner."

"Okay. I'm pulling onto the street now. Everybody stay put and don't move until I give the go ahead."

"You got ten minutes from the moment you hang up this phone to tell us something."

He ended the call, and a text came through from the kidnapper.

> 917-555-5378: Park your car and flash your headlights twice so I know it's you.

> Me: Okay.

I flashed the lights as instructed, and he texted again.

> 917-555-5378: Get out and walk inside of the park. To your left, there's the men and women's bathroom. Go into the men's bathroom and put the money in the last stall. Send a picture so that I know it's there. Once I confirm, I'll send further instruction.

Taking my phone down from the car mount, I snatched my seatbelt off and stepped out of the car. The night air hit me as I scanned the dark street, proceeding to where I'd been instructed to go. Though I'd expressed the importance of coming alone to my family, the Ruger on my hip made it so that I had company. My instincts told me that I was possibly walking into a trap, but what choice did I have? My baby needed me. And if there was one thing I knew for sure, I'd walk through the gates of hell if it meant saving my child.

I gripped the duffle bag filled with cash tightly while walking briskly. The weight of the bag was a bitter reminder that my daughter's life was put on the line for what I considered little money. I knew I was being watched. The hairs on my neck that stood up were confirmation of that. This wasn't about the cash for him no more than it was about having the upper hand. I was sure that the guy had gathered some information on me, and to have such a boss bitch moving at his command came with a thrill. However, this was no fucking game. And I planned to show him just that once I got my daughter.

The area where the bathrooms were located was eerie. The dim, yellow glow of the streetlights cast a shadow on the ground, making it appear that there were figures behind me. Still, I took a deep breath and kept moving. Making it to the door with a for men sign on it, I entered, following his directions word for word. The strong smell of piss wafted in the air, and my nose wrinkled in disgust as I counted each stall until I got to the last. With the door slightly ajar, I was able to slip the bag inside, snap a picture, and retreat outside.

With sweaty palms, I sent the picture and asked for further instructions. My heart raced when I hit send, and the delivered notification didn't pop up immediately.

"Please. Don't fuckin' do this to me," I whispered. Just as I began to panic, the notification of the delivered text popped up, and a response came immediately after.

917-555-5378: Go back to your car.

Me: Where's my daughter?

917-555-5378: Back to your car please.

Pissed, I walked back to the entrance of the park, my eyes darting around for any signs of Beautii. This nigga was playing with me. Hopping back inside the car, I slammed the door shut. I went to text the number again, and his incoming call stopped me.

"Picture someone having my kid and me not being able to follow the simple directions they gave me to get her back."

My stomach dropped, and I turned my head to see if anyone had pulled up without me giving the signal. **"What are you talkin' about? I did what you asked. Where is my daughter?"**

He snickered, and I wanted nothing more than to reach through the phone and choke his ass to death.

"See, that's the shit that gets me. Don't insult my intelligence,

Ms. Boss Bitch. I know you're here with your people. You were on the phone talking when you pulled up."

My throat tightened as I seethed from his accusations. How close was he to be able to see me on the phone? I'd been extra careful, so what was really going on? **"Listen, motherfucka, I don't know what your beef is with me, but you got your money. Stop playing games and tell me where my fuckin' child is."**

"Well, Ms. Boss Bitch, I can tell you where she would've been had you done your part. She would've been in that park." He spoke lightheartedly, but the undertone was deadly. **"And since I have to babysit again, the ransom's doubled. I'ma need 100K sooner than later. I'll hit you back with new instructions shortly."**

"You bas..." The line went dead, and I rushed out of my car back to the bathroom. There was no way he got away that fast.

"Beautii! Beautii! Baby, are you in here?" I kicked each stall open and came up empty. No money and more importantly, no Beautii.

I wanted nothing more than to fall to floor and cry. The realization that I was so close to getting her only to come up short hit me like a ton of bricks. Stomping out of the bathroom, I dialed the number back. It rang twice before going to voicemail. I called again, only for it to go straight to voicemail.

"Fuck!" I yelled out. Dialing Tiffany's number, I got back in the car.

"You got her?" she asked, answering on the first ring.

"No, Tiff! I don't have her. He got the money, and he still has Beautii!"

"We're pulling around. Stay put."

Seconds later, all three cars pulled up. Everyone got out, and I could see the guys going off in different directions. I assumed they were spreading out to search the park. I knew it was of no use. Beautii wasn't there. I couldn't feel her presence.

I rolled down the window as Tiffany, Mo, my mom, and Tionne approached.

"What did he say?" Tiff inquired.

"He knew I wasn't alone. He fuckin' knew it."

"How? We weren't even on this block. And it's dark as hell out here," Mo noted.

"He said he saw me on the phone when I pulled up."

"This car don't have tints?"

I shook my head no. "I was so fuckin' close, y'all. I just fucked it up. He still has her, and he doubled the ransom."

"Desperate." My mother pointed out. "He don't want Beautii. He want the money. And he knows so long as he has her, he can keep upping the amount."

"I'd give it all. I just need my baby."

My mother reached into the window and hugged me tight.

"The park is empty," my father announced. "Let's go back to the house and figure this out from there."

We all nodded, and Briscoe opened my passenger side door and slid inside.

"I'm riding with you."

Without putting up a fight, I put the car in drive and drove off behind the others. I had nothing more to say. I didn't want to speak anymore. I just wanted to act.

"DID YOU TRY CALLING THE NUMBER BACK?" BRISCOE ASKED as we drove back.

"I called twice. He's not answering."

"Send me the number he called you from. Somebody gon' tell me where the fuck my kid at tonight."

Picking up my phone, I forwarded the number to him. Clearly, he felt he'd do a better job at negotiating. Reaching my house, I turned the car off and got out. Bypassing everyone, I walked into the house and upstairs to Beautii's room. Locking myself inside, I sat on her bed, burying my face in one of her pillows. Though no one outside the door could do anything to comfort me, being in her space was comforting. At the same time, it fed the rage in me. And the fire burning in my chest was hot and unforgiving. I heard my phone chime in my pocket, causing me to jump up from the bed and answer it immediately.

"Hello, hello."

"Is she allergic to anything?" he asked, fucking with me.

"Can I speak to her?"

"No. Is she allergic to anything?"

"Nuts. She's allergic to nuts."

"Ohhh. Got it."

I squeezed Beautii's pillow until my knuckles cracked.

"Don't trip. She straight... for now. Just tryna get some insight of how she can go without having to cause bloodshed."

"No! Please! Don't hurt my baby."

"Have that 100K on deck. I'll call you tomorrow with a location and time. And listen this time, Mahogany, damn. A nigga running on little sleep cause I gotta watch her."

"The money isn't an issue. I'll have it."

"Aight, cool. Talk soon, Ms. Boss Bitch."

The call ended, and I could hear yelling coming from downstairs. Taking the steps two at a time, I rushed into the living room to see Tiff laid out on the floor with everyone surrounding her.

"What the hell happened?"

"She mentioned something about her chest hurting then hit the floor," Santana answered.

It seemed like chaos was happening all around me. If there was a time when I needed God to drop a silver lining, it was now.

Chapter Eleven

BRISCOE

The car ride from the failed ransom exchange was a quiet one. Out of the corner of my eye, I could see Mahogany gripping the steering wheel tightly as she drove. She hadn't said a word since I'd requested the kidnapper's number. Her jaw flexed every few seconds with her lips pressed into a flat, tight line. I knew she was replaying the scenario in her head, going over every moment from the time we left her place to the moment we got to the location, silently searching for answers that wouldn't change a damn thing.

The fact was her need to do things her way had cost us. We hadn't even seen Beautii. She hadn't demanded physical proof of life before just handing over the bag of money. While Beautii's life was the ultimate leverage on the kidnapper's end, we'd given up the only leverage we had. And now, he wanted more. The money was never the issue. What burned me up inside was the fact that this bitch ass nigga had scored another opportunity to dangle our child over our heads again.

Mahogany's need to take the reins, her tendency to move on her own instincts alone, was nothing new. I'd known all about it before I fell in love and bore a child with her. In the beginning of our relationship, I admired it. But tonight? Tonight had taken a turn, starting from the shit

77

with Coolie until now. Everyone was quick to point out how harsh I was in my delivery, but no one wanted to speak on the facts.

Every quiet part of me was yelling at her pride in the moment. Her inability to step back and listen to me had just cost us our best chance at getting our daughter back. The urge to tell her that had the words caught up in my throat before they could fully come out. Even in the moment where my heart was shredded, I had the small amount of decency to know that now wasn't the time. I wouldn't express my judgement out loud, though I was judging her and the family like a motherfucka.

The silence that filled the car wasn't helping at all. The closer we got to her house, the louder my frustration became in my own head. But what the hell could I do in the moment? Taking a final look over at her, her shoulders were now slumped as we pulled into her driveway. Without exchanging any further words with me, she turned off the engine and got out of the car. I stayed in the passenger seat, watching as everyone did the same with Coolie, Dough, and this random ass nigga, Justice, walking in last.

That was another thing that had me fucked up regarding her decision making, her bringing complete strangers into the fold but wanting me to be mindful of who I enlisted for help. I didn't give a fuck that this nigga had ties to the Wright family. I didn't know him nor did I know her long lost brother. And the fact that my vote wasn't even casted as to how much these niggas could or should be included on had me feeling less like Beautii's father and more like a distant relative. Which was why I was pushing the issue of having the direct number to the kidnapper myself.

Getting out of Mahogany's car, I jogged over to my own. Once inside, I hit call for the number she'd given me and placed the call on speakerphone. I listened as it rang once, twice, then three times before cutting to voicemail. No name, no generic information in the automated message. Nothing. I called once more and got the same result.

"Bitch ass nigga," I muttered under my breath, disgusted with the cowardness of the kidnapper.

Dropping my phone in the cupholder, I started my car and pulled out of the driveway. Mahogany might've been running her own version of what the search was supposed to look like, but as Beautii's father, it was my turn to take the lead. No sooner than I turned off of Mahogany's street, my phone vibrated. Seeing my shorty, Mia's name on the screen, I sighed. I'd been putting her on the backburner since finding out Beautii was missing. I hadn't told her what was going on because, quite frankly, it was none of her business. Still, as I drove, I answered the call, just to let her know that I'd be off the grid for a couple days.

"Well, hey, stranger. You forgot about little ol' me." She spoke in a sarcastic tone.

"Nah. I just got a lot going on right now. I answered to let you know that."

"Anything I can help with?"

"Nah. It's some family stuff."

"Oh," she replied, sounding salty. **"Well, alright. I guess call me when they find your daughter."** She whispered the last part, at least she thought she did, but I heard it loud and clear.

"What the fuck you just say?"

"Huh?"

"Mia, I will have someone at your door in five minutes, kicking that bitch off the hinges. What... the... fuck... did you just say?" I gritted.

"I said call me when you find your daughter," she replied nervously.

"Find my daughter? What the fuck are you talkin' about?" I wasn't giving her any information that she could piggyback on. I wanted to know what she knew.

"I... I... I overheard you talkin' earlier today."

"Heard me when?"

"When I called you. You must've thought you declined the call, but you answered it, and I heard you mention to someone about your daughter being missing since last night."

Enraged, I sat the phone down in my lap to avoid launching it. **"So, in you knowing what you think you know, you still thought it was cool to call me talkin' this bullshit about forgettin' about you?"**

"No, bae. It wasn't like that. I was ju..."

"Just being inconsiderate as fuck. Get off my line fore I do something to you, Mia," I threatened.

"Briscoe, wai..."

"What the fuck I say?!"

The call ended abruptly, and I shook my head. I didn't know what the fuck Mia had going on, but she did not want to be on my suspect list. Anybody there was as good as dead.

Finding myself at my brother, L.A.'s front door, I knocked. My adrenaline had burned through all the patience I had left, so when he didn't answer after the first knock, I banged on the door.

"What the fuck, nigga?" he spat, snatching it open. "You tryna have the neighbors calling the cops and shit?"

"Why you ain't answer the first fuckin' time? I know you heard me through these thin ass walls." I let myself in and heard him close the door behind me.

"If you must know, I was taking a shit. And what the fuck happened to your lip?"

I'd been so preoccupied, my swollen lip from the sucker punch Coolie threw my way was the last thing on my mind. "Don't worry about that."

Inside, I looked around and frowned at the mess. It smelled fresh, but L.A. just never had a knack for cleaning up.

"Stop looking round my shit like you bout to steal something. Wassup? Y'all find Beautii?"

I whipped my head around in his direction as he lit up a blunt. "Nigga, you think I'd be here if we did? No. And that nigga got the money and my kid, man."

"What? How the fu... You know what? Nevermind. What you need from me, big bro?"

Pulling out my burner phone, I went to the number I'd called and handed it over. "This the number that the person used to call Mahogany. Can you run it, ping it, or do whatever it is that y'all techy niggas do?"

L.A. took a pull of his blunt and took the phone from me. "You mean to tell me they didn't do this shit when they first got the call?"

"They did. And they couldn't find anything. I need you to do it. It's always good to cross check."

"I got you." He went over to his computer and powered it on.

As he worked, I sat down and scrolled the photo gallery in my personal phone. I had one filled with pictures of Beautii from the moment she was born to her last birthday. As I analyzed each picture, the pain amplified. I had to find my daughter. I knew she was somewhere waiting for me and Mahogany to make it happen, and I knew we would. It just seemed like we were on the losing end of the race against the clock.

"You and Mahogany good?" L.A. asked, breaking the silence as he tapped away at the keys.

"Define good," I said dryly, locking my phone and looking over at him.

"I mean good where y'all working together to make sure Beautii is back home safely."

I scoffed. "Mahogany don't know shit about working together. All she knows is her way or no way."

"Like you."

"Nah. Not like me."

"Exactly like you. That's why y'all always bumping heads. It's the reason why you're here having me run this number. Y'all like to do shit y'all own way. And any other time, that might be cool, but at a crucial time such as this one, y'all should be moving in sync. There shouldn't be no your way and her way."

"Yeah, well, tell her stubborn ass that. Her way is what got us here. Did you find anything?"

Spinning around in his chair, he handed me my phone back. "It pinged one time in this area but nothing else after that."

I got closer to the screen and recognized the area from the street view. "That's where the meet up place was. Fuck!" I yelled out in frustration because we still had nothing. "He doubled the ransom after he skated off."

"So, y'all have another chance."

"Yeah. And it may be our last one."

"Aight. Send me the info once you get it, and I'll be around."

"Preciate that."

"Bro, remember, Beautii has two parents. She's counting on both of y'all."

"I know. I'm gonna head back over to her crib now. Good looking, bro."

Leaving L.A.'s place, the shit Mia said to me kept playing over in my head. I knew I should've headed back to Mahogany's, but my car had a mind of its own and ventured into the Washington PJs in the Bronx where she lived. Parking in the lot behind the building, I hopped out. Passing a bunch of young niggas that littered the benches, I popped the front door to get into the lobby.

Skipping the pissy elevators, I took the steps two at a time up to her third-floor apartment. Navigating to apartment 3B, I banged on the door. It didn't take her long to answer. And that was typical. Anyone banging that hard on your door and you living in the PJs, you'd wanna come see what it was about.

"Who is it?! Banging on my goddamn door like that!"

"It's B, Mia." I made sure to keep my voice calm so that she would think I came in peace.

"Briscoe, baby. I'm..." As soon as she opened the door, I grabbed her by her neck and pushed her back, kicking the door closed. "Bri..." She tried to speak, but my grip was too tight.

"Tell me what you know about my daughter, Mia. And if I even sense you lyin', I'ma end yo ass, and I promise they won't find yo body for days."

She shook her head wildly. I loosened my grip to let her speak. Gasping dramatically, big tears fell down her face. "I don't know, Briscoe. I swear to God; I don't know anything. Please."

Seeing the sincerity in her eyes, I let her go. "This shit over! You sneaky, and I can't trust you. That ear hustling shit almost got yo' ass killed."

I stared down at her for a second while she inched back from me on the floor and felt a twinge of regret. But I had no sorries to give, so I left as quiet as I had come. Taking the steps back down to my car, I got inside and sat for a minute. I had to get my thoughts together. I wanted my daughter back so bad, I was moving erratically. After a couple minutes, I started the car and went to pull out when I saw flashing lights and heard police sirens. Knowing their arrival had nothing to do with me, I kept moving, only to be stopped by a cop car swerving in front of mine.

Confused, I put the car in park and threw my hands up. These niggas weren't gon' kill me.

"Out of the car and on the ground. NOW!" I heard.

Complying, I got out, ready to plead my case of obvious mistaken identity. "Fuck is going on?"

"What's your name?"

"How y'all just tell a nigga to get on the ground, and I don't know what's going on?"

"Name?!"

"Bryon Smalls."

"Bryon Smalls, you're under arrest for assault with a deadly weapon."

"The fuck? I ain't assault nobody."

"Mia Kinsley," he let out, and I dropped my head.

Did this weak ass bitch have the boys on speed dial? How the fuck was I gonna explain this shit to Mahogany?

Chapter Twelve

RAZOR

I moved with purpose, slipping through the dark alleyways that I remembered from childhood until I was back on the street where my car sat parked. Entering the car, I placed the duffle bag in the passenger seat with one destination in mind — the Airbnb. This game was chess not checkers, and every move I made had to be well thought out and with a purpose. Hence the reason I decided at the last minute that there would be no exchange. Not one that included me handing the kid over. Not now at least. I'd picked the drop off location because it was a place I knew like the back of my hand. There were different cuts that I could hide out in and watch Mahogany drop off the money at the same time.

I looked on as the family gathered around her car and did a sweep of the park, only to come up empty. My dark skin blended well under the night sky, helping me go undetected. I still couldn't believe that she thought I would hand over the leverage of a lifetime for fifty thousand dollars. That wouldn't have put a dent in her pockets. The Wright family's Table had been fed by block money for over a decade with Mahogany upping their fortune with her club. And having been Santana's best friend since middle school, I'd seen the come up first-hand. I also kept my ears to the streets all the way from Cali.

I'd be a fool to believe that Mahogany didn't have stacks on top of stacks hidden away to keep her empire going. But I wasn't no fool by a longshot. I had no intentions on giving her kid back for fifty racks. She had a bag, and I wanted to see how much I could tax her. Doubling the ransom sounded good enough to me, so that was just what I did. As I drove, I smiled at the way things had played out thus far. Santana was none the wiser, and then there was Renee — perfect, calculating Renee who just wanted some attention and a good dick down.

"The perfect sneaky link," I muttered.

She'd played her part well. It was because of her calculating and manipulative ways that I was able to keep tabs on Santana. She'd convinced him to share his location with her after their first run in with Mahogany's people. Renee didn't know it, but she'd assisted with my plan to snatch Beautii up without even knowing. It was because of her tracking that I was able to get the address to his mother's house. It was also how I knew beforehand that Mahogany hadn't come to the drop alone.

Keeping track of Santana's location, giving me insight on what she knew about Mahogany's next move, that was the kind of loyalty I needed at the moment. I had no reason to think she wouldn't remain loyal, especially since she'd shown her face to Beautii. Beautii had seen everything. All it would take was for Mahogany to put two and two together, and Renee was as good as dead. She knew opening her mouth about me would only be the nail in her coffin. That was why I trusted her — to an extent.

Hopping on the expressway back to the Airbnb, I decided to reach out to Santana. We hadn't touched bases, and I wanted to see where his head was at, check his temperature a little. Navigating my recent call list, I received a text message from my contact.

MoneyMove: Did she deliver?

Me: She did.

MoneyMove: And you got the money?

Me: Yep.

MoneyMove: What about the kid?

Me: Still in my custody.

MoneyMove: …we're gonna hold onto her as long as we can. She's the way in. I have something else I'm working on in the meantime. Stay by your phone.

Me: Aight.

Pressing Santana's contact, the phone rang a few times. By the fourth ring, I went to hang up, and he answered.

"Yo."

"Wassup, man? Haven't heard from you. What's the move?"

"Dawg, it's a lot going on right now. A lot. I'm still working from the inside though."

"What you mean a lot going on? They got you putting in work?"

He sighed. "Nah. Family stuff."

"Family stuff?" I repeated sourly.

"Yeah. But I'm wrapping something up. Lemme hit you back."

"Aight, man. Yo, hol' up. What's the timeframe on us heading back home?"

"Soon as I get the word that shit is in motion, bruh. I got ears right now. Lemme slide."

He hung up, and I shook my head. Him mentioning family and not including me in those plans drew a line in the sand, further confirming that Santana was out for self, so I had to look out for Razor.

FINALLY MAKING IT BACK TO THE AIRBNB, THE LIGHTS WERE out like I'd left them. Setting the duffle bag on the floor in the living room, I went to check on Beautii. Walking inside the small bedroom, I turned to the closet to open it. She was right where I'd stashed her, her wrists and ankles tied and gagged with a silk scarf I'd found in one of the dresser drawers. She looked up once she heard the door open.

Her eyes were wide and sharp, indicating that she was pissed. And though her tear-streaked face was evidence of her crying, I could see she wasn't broken yet. I had to give it to her. Even though she was being raised a princess, she was a Wright through and through. Quiet, yes, but there was something calculating behind her eyes, like she was waiting for her moment to strike or escape. Unfortunately for her, I wasn't going to give room for that to happen.

"It looks like you'll be with me another night," I said, taking off my coat and tossing it on a nearby chair in the room. Her head shaking was followed by a muffled response that made me shrug my shoulders. "Yeah, yeah, I know. The babysitting shit ain't my thing either, so the feeling is mutual, shorty. You hungry, thirsty?"

She gave a muffled reply to which I pulled the scarf down enough for her to speak clearly.

"I gotta use the bathroom."

"Aight. Remember how we made this work the last time. I'll be right outside the door once you're done." Placing the scarf back on her mouth, I helped her up from the floor.

Escorting her to the bathroom in the hallway, I used my blade to cut off the zip tie from her hands. She rubbed her wrists that appeared to be slightly bruised due to the tightness of the zip tie. I made a note to loosen it a little once she was done. Closing the door to give her privacy, I set the stopwatch on my phone to two minutes. It was more than enough time for her to empty her bladder. The timer started, and my phone rang. It was Renee.

"Wassup?"

"Hey. Can you talk?"

"Briefly."

"Okay. I'll make it quick. Me and Asia need to come over there. You think you can extend the time on the Airbnb?"

I heard the toilet flush, and I knocked on the door twice to make sure she was done. She knocked back as a signal that she was. I opened the door, and she stood there with her hands outstretched to me. Taking out a new pair of zip ties, I put them on and made sure that they were loose enough to take the pressure off her wrists but still effective. Taking her back to the room, I let her sit in the chair and turned on the TV to keep her company.

"Razor, you there?"

"Yeah," I replied, walking into the living room.

"So, can we come over there?"

"Has Asia met Beautii?"

"Yeah."

"Well, then, how that shit gon' work? You know how close Asia is with her dad. She tell that nigga everything." Silence filled the line.

"I'll deal with Asia. Right now, it sounds like you're making excuses. Just say no if you don't want us there."

"If you don't get outta here with all that dramatic bullshit. I'm over here tryna make sure my ass is covered."

Sighing dramatically, Renee responded. **"I wanna make sure the same thing. I told you it's us against everybody. Santana got here and forgot about me and his child. You're all I got, Razor."**

Closing my eyes, I pinched the bridge of my nose. Although I was using Renee, I couldn't let her feel it, so I gave in. **"Aight. Come on. If you fuck this up for me, Renee…"**

"I won't, bae. I promise."

Ending the call, I tossed the burner phone on the couch. Renee had just thrown a monkey wrench in my plans, trying to lowkey throw some family shit on me. I wasn't her savior, and after all was said and done, I had no real plans for us. She'd served her purpose, and I'd be damned if I waited around for her to do me how she was currently doing Santana. I wasn't tender dick bout no ho.

Making myself comfortable on the couch and mentally preparing for her arrival, I thought about where I'd set up the new meet up spot for Mahogany. The drop had to be as perfect as the one tonight. 100K was on the line.

Chapter Thirteen

SANTANA

The way shit had been unraveling over the last twelve hours felt more like a slow-motion car crash rather than real life. Since I'd found my way in, chaos seemed to be the only constant. Not only were we still on the hunt for Beautii, but now we were down a link in the chain. One minute, Tiffany was standing with us, and the next, she was clutching her chest and falling to the ground. Everything from there happened so fast that if I blinked, I knew I would've missed something.

Dough swooped her up in his arms and bolted out the door. He didn't ask the ETA on the ambulance Mo had called, just ran like a madman to his car, doing what any other father would have done for their child. We all scrambled to follow him, everyone hopping in their separate cars, pulling off in a fleet like lineup, en route to the hospital. It was another hit that we couldn't afford.

While everyone rushed off, it was Morae who dragged behind, seemingly breaking apart at the seams. I was already halfway to my car when I heard her screaming.

"Where the fuck are the keys?!" Her voice cracked under panic and frustration.

Seeing her frustrated and fumbling with every step she took, I could've left her there to figure it out, but my feet wouldn't allow me to move forward. I had to remind myself that we were in this shit together and on the same team. "Aye, I can drive you. Come on," I offered sincerely.

Snapping her head in my direction, she replied with ice in her tone. "I don't need you to do shit for me, Santana!"

"Well, as you can see, everybody done pulled the fuck off," I shot back, my tone matching hers. I motioned to the empty driveway. "You wanna stand here yelling, or you wanna make it to the hospital?"

We had a stare off, and for a split second, I caught a flash of regret in her eyes. Then, she blinked, and just as quickly, that hard glare was back. Her ringing phone caught her attention, and she turned away from me as she answered.

"Yeah, bro."

She paused, allowing the person on the line to speak before giving an account of what happened with Tiff. I could hear the person's voice clearly as they yelled into the phone. I assumed it was her brother, Money. I'd concluded that he and Tiffany were a thing back at the warehouse. When Mo's head dropped, she confirmed my assumption.

"I'm headed there now, Montez! Stop yellin' at me!" Hanging up the phone, I watched her shoulders rise and fall.

"Come on," I encouraged, walking over to my rental.

She stood still for a few seconds before making her way over to the passenger side of the car. By the time I got behind the wheel, she was buckled up, arms crossed tightly over her chest and her face turned toward the window. "Westchester Medical," she said.

"You gotta give me the address, Ma. I'll type it into the GPS."

Without responding, she leaned forward and typed the name of the hospital into the navigation system.

"Get us there quick please."

"I got you."

Out of the trio, Morae seemed the most closed off. She was tough and had a *don't fuck with me* persona about her. The woman that sat across from me tonight was the complete opposite. Still, she was doing everything in her power not to crumble beside me. I glanced at her out of the corner of my eye and tried a different approach.

"She gon' be straight, Mo. She gon' thug this shit off and be right back on the frontline in no time," I said, keeping my eyes on the road.

"Don't do that."

"Do what?"

"Don't sit here and feed me some bullshit about how she's gonna be good as a way to try to get in good with me, Santana. We are on the same team, but you ain't a part of this shit."

My grip tightened on the steering wheel to control my anger. Similar to my sister, Mo had a mouth on her. Shit, they all did. That was where women had me fucked up. It made me think back to Renee and that shit she was spitting at the hotel. I had to leave to keep from smacking her head against the wall.

"I'm just tryna give yo ass some encouraging words. You ain't gotta lash out at me cause you scared."

"Who said anything about being scared?" she questioned, now facing me. "You don't know shit about what I'm feeling right now. But since we're on the subject, lemme tell you what I feel about you. I feel that you either knowingly brought your bullshit here, or it followed you. No need to overplay your role to prove to me anything different either. My mind is already made up, and the truth will come to light soon."

Something inside me snapped at her implication that I was the sole reason for the chaos. Sure, I'd started out with my own plan, but it never included kidnapping. Even my thoughts of pushing Mahogany out of her spot didn't end with any of the ladies dying. The patience that I had reserved for her emotional state had dissipated just that quick.

"You think a nigga over here playing? I ain't have to stop for yo' ass, Mo. Everybody else dipped, remember?"

"Because I told them to," she countered. "Be clear on that."

"Nah, you be clear on the fact that you in my shit talkin' crazy. Yet the only thing standing between you and getting to this hospital right now is me. I don't give a fuck about y'all's' respect. I've earned my stripes. Got me fucked up if you think I'm out this bitch lookin' for dog treats for being a solid ass nigga!" My voice bounced off the windows in the car, but she sat quietly, unfazed.

When I finally pulled up to the hospital's entrance, Morae was unbuckling her seatbelt before the car came to a full stop. Once she was out, I barely waited for her to step back before I pressed down on the gas, tires squealing as I took off. At this point, I could give a fuck about how my absence made me look. I had my own family to look after too.

———

I CALLED RENEE ON MY WAY TO THE HOTEL TO SEE WHERE her head was at. I wasn't in the mood to be arguing. The last thing she'd want to do was pick a fight with me at this time anyway. I was still blown about her leaving Asia at the hotel alone. That shit blew my mind. I didn't know why she thought it was okay considering the current climate. And her being so nonchalant about it really made me want to yoke her ass up.

Though she had every right to be in her feelings about what happened at Mahogany's house, moving sloppy as a result of it was green as fuck. Her phone rang a few times before the voicemail picked up. Not surprised, I hung up, and a few seconds later, the phone rang. Thinking it was Renee, I was surprised to see my father's name on the screen. The last time we spoke, he wasn't happy about the direction I chose to go in with my plan. We hadn't spoken since then. With a headache on the rise, I answered the call, prepared to hang up if he was on bullshit.

"**Wassup, Pop?**" I forced out.

"**Shit, I was hoping you could tell me. What's going on witcha?**"

"**Nothing at the moment. Still working some shit out. I'll be heading back home soon though. We're setting up shop out there. Got a lot put in motion.**"

He snickered. "**We, huh? Does that we consist of your sister and her people? Let me guess, you couldn't get the whole pie, so you settled for a piece of it? You really went up top and let them Wrights play you, boy.**"

"Fuck is you talkin' bout? Ain't nobody played me."

"Shiiddd, let you tell it. Lemme ask you this. Where's Razor? You know, ya boy that you're supposed to be coordinating all this with."

"He around. He knows what's going on."

"Well, since you got everything covered, I guess I'll see you whenever you touch down."

"Uh huh," I replied, ready to end the conversation.

"You just remember, son. You're a Coast. Not a Wright. We take what we want. We don't wait for a motherfucka to give it to us. Be safe out there." He hung up, and I closed my eyes tight and massaged my temples.

There was always some underlying shit with my father. I'd seen how he'd mind fucked people firsthand growing up. Not only had I watched, but I'd learned and became a pro at the shit myself. He ended the call with that last statement for a reason. I was just too overwhelmed with thoughts at the moment to figure it out right now, so I stored it to come back to later.

Parking the car, I entered the hotel and took the elevators straight upstairs to the room. There was only one thing that could stop the pounding in my head, and I hoped that Renee could put her head to the side to handle it for me. I needed her to suck the stress outta me. A nigga needed clarity in the worst way. Using my keycard to gain entry, the first thing that hit me was stillness. The room was quiet, and all the lights were turned off.

"Renee," I called out, flicking the closest light on. When I didn't get a response, my heart raced. "Renee! Asia!" I yelled out, searching both bedrooms only to find each one empty.

Calming myself as best I could, I pulled out my phone to dial Renee again. It rang... and rang... and rang. Then, voicemail. I cursed under my breath and tried three more times, but each result was the same. I then called Asia, whose phone didn't ring at all. *What the fuck is going on?* I thought to myself as I checked for their luggage, that was untouched. The only thing missing in the room was the two of them and the things they could carry by hand.

Rushing back out the door, I went downstairs to question the front desk personnel.

"Excuse me," I spoke as I approached the desk. "Did you happen to see a brown skin woman with a short haircut leave out with a young girl about ye high?" I put my hand up to my chest in an effort to give a measurement of how tall Asia was. "The young girl would've had a bun in her hair. A puffy one."

The woman watched me intently, as if she were trying to visualize who I was referring to. "Umm, honestly, sir, I just started my shift about five minutes ago, and I've seen a bunch of people in and out. Lemme ask my coworker. She's been here since earlier this afternoon."

"Aight, thanks." As she walked away, I went to call Renee again, and the voicemail picked up.

"Hi, how can I help you?" an older woman asked with a smile.

"Hey. I'm in room 2122, and I'm tryna locate my wife and daughter." She gave me a confused look, letting me know I had to say something that made more sense to her. "My wife is bipolar, and I just wanna make sure she and my daughter are safe," I lied. "She left her phone in the room, and my daughter's phone is going straight to voicemail."

"Ohhh. I completely understand. Can you give me their descriptions again?"

I ran down their descriptions and what I remembered Asia having on.

"You said room 2112, right?"

"Yes."

"Okay. One second cause I think I checked her out."

"Checked her out?" I repeated, my heart thumping.

She typed on her computer and turned the screen around. "Yes. That was her. She said she was checking out but to still keep the room in the system as occupied for the other guest. Which I'm assuming was you."

"Okay, thank you." Turning swiftly, I headed for the exit.

"Sir, wait! I can call someone..."

Her voice trailed off as I pushed the door open and rushed back to my car. There was no way Renee just left with Asia, leaving everything behind. Someone had to have coached her to handle things the way she did. Did the same person that got to Beautii manage to snatch my family up while I was out trying to be the hero in The Table's story? Uneasy about who I could depend on to help me, I made a call to the one person I felt like I could trust. The phone rang once, and they picked up.

"Hello?"

"Ma, I need you."

Chapter Fourteen

MORAE

The hospital felt more like a prison than a place of comfort. As we all stood by and waited on an update on Tiffany's condition, the beige walls felt like they were closing in on me. My knees bounced nervously as I checked my phone periodically for a call or text from Money to let me know how close he was. He barely let me get many words out without yelling after I let him know what was going on with Tiff. They'd rushed her to the back not long before I arrived according to Mahogany. She sat next to me, looking off into space, and I didn't have to imagine what was going through her head as I was sure that my thoughts mirrored hers.

"They said something about cardiac arrest and her BP dropping," Mahogany spoke. "How the hell did she go into cardiac arrest, Mo? What did we miss? What didn't she tell us?"

If she was looking for me to answer those questions, I refused. *She said she was okay,* I thought to myself. "I don't know, Hogany," I uttered out loud.

My eyes kept darting toward the swinging doors of the ER, hoping the next doctor or nurse that came through was headed in our direction with news but nothing so far. I looked across the room at Tiffany's parents and shook my head. Dough sat up straight, stone faced, while his wife lay on his shoulder, occasionally patting her eyes dry of the tears that fell. The weight of it all, the guilt of knowing, was suffocating. I let her push herself and talk herself into thinking that showing up in pain counted for something. I should've forced her to sit this one out. Instead, I trusted her instinct, even though, deep down, I knew better.

Just as my head dropped, I heard my name called.

"Mo!"

My head shot up when I recognized Money's voice. He weaved his way through the crowded waiting room and over to me like a man possessed. When he reached me, I didn't even get a chance to speak. His eyes bore into mine, not angry but frantic.

"What they saying? Where she at?"

"They took her to the back, Money." Hogany spoke on my behalf. "Here, sit down."

"I don't wanna sit down. I need to know what's going on. Anybody talked to a doctor yet?"

"Not yet." Hogany continued to answer. "Her parents are here, so they'll likely talk to them first."

"Why you ain't sayin' shit, Morae?" he snapped at me. "You not sayin' shit is telling me there's more I need to know."

"She..." I paused to swallow the lump in my throat. "She said she was having chest pain earlier. I asked if she'd taken her medicine, and she said no because she didn't like the way the pain pills made her feel."

Mahogany shook her head, and Money took a step back, scrubbing a hand over his face. For a moment, he stood there in front of me, trying to absorb what I'd just said. While I didn't want to speak on the situation with Mahogany, I couldn't lie to him about the love of his life. He clenched his jaw so tight, I thought his teeth might crack.

"What else is going on?"

Mahogany and I looked back-and-forth between each other before turning back to him. "Come outside real quick," she said to him.

We walked outside, and Money stood in front of us, arms folded, waiting for either one of us to speak.

I took the initiative. "Paris is gone."

"And Beautii is missing," Mahogany added.

"All this shit happened over the course of the twenty-four hours I've been gone? When Beautii go missing? Whose out on the streets? Paris missing too?"

"No, Money. Paris is dead," I replied, and the words made my mouth dry.

"Dead?" he echoed, his voice filled with disbelief. "What happened?"

I opened my mouth to respond, but before I could, commotion broke out as nurses and doctors came rushing through the ER doors, pushing a gurney. Security personnel were directly behind them.

"Excuse me," security spoke. "Y'all gotta clear the area."

The three of us moved from the front entrance just as the ambulance swerved into the entryway of the hospital. By the way they moved with haste, whoever was set to come out of the truck must've been of some level of importance. We looked on as the doors swung open, and they quickly transferred the person.

"We have a GSW to the chest," the paramedic informed. "We need to get him to the operating room STAT!"

As the doctors and nurses swarmed the figure on the gurney, I was able to catch a glimpse of the person on the oxygen mask.

"Dudas?" The name shot out of my mouth before my brain could compute.

Money turned toward me sharply. "Dudas? Ain't no way that's Maurice, man."

Neither of us waited for confirmation. Moving in sync, we followed the people as they rushed inside.

"Wait," I spoke up. "I think that's my brother," I managed to get out before they pushed through the double doors labeled Trauma Unit.

My stomach turned, and I hoped that my mind was playing tricks on me.

"What the fuck is going on?!" Money exploded, his voice loud enough to draw attention.

"Sir, please," one of the hospital staff said to Money. "We can't have that in here."

"He's fine," Mahogany assured, pulling Money to the side. "We got him. Listen, you can't be in this hospital blacking out like that. They gon' put yo' ass out. Let me go see if they have any information on the person that came in. We can't move on assumptions. I'll be back."

Mahogany walked off, leaving us both to our thoughts.

The moment I caught that glimpse, I knew it was my brother. The side profile was all I needed. My brothers all had distinct features, and Dudas had one of those faces you couldn't mistake. I would've known him anywhere.

"Mo, you sure it was Dudas on that gurney?" Money asked again. Hope filled his voice.

I nodded, though I wanted with every fiber of my being to be wrong. "It's him, Montez."

Money said nothing after that, just clenched his fists at his sides, closed his eyes, and paced. I'd seen him the same way when our mom passed. Between the unknown of Tiffany's condition and now Dudas, the pressure of it was just too much.

"What's going on?" I looked up to see Mahogany's mom walking toward us. "Hey, Montez. I didn't know you were here, baby." Without an invitation, she stopped him from pacing and pulled him in for a hug I knew he needed. "Tiff is gonna be fine, baby. Just fine."

I could see Mahogany make her way back over to us with a solemn look on her face. I turned away, placing my body against the wall to hold me up.

"It's him," she confirmed quietly. "It's Dudas. He was shot three times in the chest,' she continued, her voice trembling as she spoke. "They... they said it don't look good."

"It don't look good? How the fuck it don't look good?! They can't count him out! They don't have the last say."

I overheard Annette on the phone with Coolie as she did her best to calm Money. Not wanting him to get kicked out, I pulled him by his shirt and into a hug. I could barely hold myself together, but a voice in the back of my head said to hold it down like my mom had taught me. I was the glue. Money pulled away from me and threw his head back, likely hiding his tears. Coolie, Dough, Tionne, and Justice rounded the corner at the same time the doors to the Trauma Unit swung open, and two doctors walked out. They didn't have to call for the family for me to know the news they were going to deliver, but they did anyway.

"Family of Maurice Thompson."

We all started in their direction, surrounding the two doctors once we were close.

"We're the family of Maurice."

The clear face doctor nodded before speaking. "We did all that we could to save him. Unfortunately, one of the bullets hit a main artery, and we couldn't get the bleeding under control. We're sorry for your loss." The words were rehearsed, but the empathy was felt.

The news was enough to knock me off my feet. Dudas was dead. My brother was gone. And no one could tell us anymore than that. Coolie thanked the doctors, and they walked off.

"Family of Tiffany Richards."

Tiffany's parents walked over to her doctors while my feet stayed planted. Money didn't even move. The shock of losing a sibling had us in a different state of mind. Out of the corner of my eye, I could see Tiffany's mother throw her hands up and Dough shake the doctor's hand, and I assumed they'd received good news. I thanked God that she was okay.

"We gotta go see Dad," Money finally spoke.

"I know," I said, getting choked up. It was the last thing I wanted to do, but I knew it was news he'd only wanna hear from us.

***

I felt like I was on autopilot as I walked to Money's car. My legs moved on their own, but my mind remained frozen, back in the waiting area where the doctor had delivered the final blow. Dudas was dead. Vivid images of his stern facial expression when he called himself trying to reprimand me as a child popped in my head. Out of my three brothers, I gave him hell the most from childhood up until now. And it was never because I had an issue with him but because I'd always had this boss like tendency about me, and my older brother couldn't take that. I remembered him always coming to my defense at school when I wouldn't let the bullies have their way. Dudas was my protector when I allowed him to be.

I slid into the passenger seat of Money's car without a word.

Closing the door harder than necessary, he started the engine but didn't move. The air was thick between us, neither of us wanting to acknowledge the weight of the pain. Though there were cars parked throughout the parking lot, it felt as if just me and Money existed. I reached over to squeeze his hand reassuringly, and he put the car in drive.

"I don't even know how to tell him, Mo." Money's voice was low and raw. "When we pull up to the house... what are we supposed to say?"

My heart sank even deeper. I'd already been the bearer of bad news with Ms. Reece, and now I had to tell my father that his oldest son was no longer with us. I stared out the window, watching the city blur past, with people along the streets so vividly alive, uncaring that my world was merely falling apart right in front of my eyes.

"I don't know," I admitted, my voice barely above a whisper. "Dad... he'll be strong for us. It's who he is. He defines strength. At the same time, Dudas was his firstborn. His **firstborn**. That's going to hit him different."

"And Monk Man. Before he and I had a bond, Dudas was his go to."

"Yeah. That's until Dudas started actin' like Daddy. Monk Man said fuck that shit." I giggled a little through my tears.

"Deadass." Money chuckled. "Dudas couldn't teach my young nigga how to be a player."

Sharing in a lighthearted laugh briefly chipped away at the heaviness that filled the car. The remainder of the ride, we were both confined to our thoughts. Mine consisted of trying to digest the last twelve hours of my life. Paris. Dudas. Mahogany and her missing daughter. Everything felt like an avalanche that I was pinned under. And yet, the exhausted voice in the back of my head kept ringing, **hold it down. Hold it down**. If I broke completely, I knew I couldn't keep my family together, and that was my job.

When we pulled up to the house, my stomach twisted. *Be the glue, Morae. That's what Mommy left you here to be.* I coached myself with each step I took until we were at the front door of our family home. Money went to take out his key, and the door was opened before he could use it. Monk Man stood on the other side of it with red eyes.

"It's true, ain't it?" he questioned, as if confirmation from us would be the only way he believed what he'd been told.

"Yes," I spoke carefully. "We just left the hospital." Lowering his head, he stepped back to let us inside. "Where's Dad?"

"In his office."

I took the lead while Monk Man and Money followed behind me. My dad's office door was closed. Sensing our presence, he called out for us to come inside. He sat at his desk with one hand balled into a fist on the table and the other up to his mouth.

"They say he was shot while on duty," he finally spoke, his voice hollow. "One of the detectives just left here. Someone killed my son. Tell me how the most sought out detective in New York gets shot up and killed in his own damn car?" He looked up at us, and his face was filled with grief and rage wrapped together so tightly that it looked as if he were fighting to breathe through it.

That was when an idea hit me. "Monk. Do you still have access to Dudas' personal dashcam for his car that he gave you?"

"Yeah. I can run it now. Gimmie ten minutes." Rushing out, he left us with my dad.

"I'ma figure this shit out, Daddy. All of it. I promise."

He nodded but remained silent.

"Let's give him a minute," Money said, leaving the room.

Agreeing, we walked out, closing the door behind us. "I think you should go back to the hospital and sit with Tiff. There's not much we can do here now. I'm gonna hit Mahogany to find out the move for Beautii and likely stay the night here."

"One of us gotta stay here. I know Pops wouldn't want us hovering, but we just need to be in close proximity."

"Right. Hit me once you get to the hospital, so I know you got there safe."

"My safety is the last thing you need to be worried about. You need to be worried about the safety of any motherfucka that try me tonight." Kissing my forehead, Money left out the house.

I secured the alarm and headed for Monk Man's room. Knocking before entering, I found him at his computer.

"I got in," he said, pointing to the screen where the video was paused.

"Press play," I pushed.

The video played, and we could see Dudas stepping out of his car and approaching what looked like a Lexus LS. He knocked on the windshield of the driver's side door and exchanged words with the driver. Although it was dark, the headlights from his car gave us a clear view of what was going on. In a split second, Dudas took two steps back, and shots rang out from the Lexus. Three shots in total hit his chest before the car skated off.

"Where was he?" I questioned, trying to get myself together. Monk Man was quiet as he stared at the screen, and that bothered me. "Monroe, where is the location on the dashboard?"

He turned slightly with tear filled eyes. "Your apartment."

My apartment? What the hell was he doing at my place? Who was at my place that would want to kill him? As the questions came to me at a rapid pace, I immediately called Mahogany. I needed answers because right now, it felt like I was the ultimate target.

Chapter Fifteen

RAZOR

THE ENGINE OF THE CAR HUMMED AS I SHOT DOWN THE NEAR abandoned streets and swerved onto the highway. Renee sat stiff in the passenger seat, her hands trembling violently as if her body was trying to reject the reality of what just went down. Suddenly, her hand spasmed, and the still-smoking gun slipped from her hand, hitting the floormat with a loud thud. My foot instinctively mashed harder on the gas as my head shot to the side.

"What the fuck?!" I barked, the anger searing out of me. The sharp scent of gunpowder still lingered in the air. Prying my eyes from the road, I glared at her. "Man, you crazy as fuck! That shit could've gone off!"

Her wide, bloodshot eyes darted to me as though she couldn't process my words. Turning on the light in the car, I could see her chest rise and fall rapidly. She was in shock. I could've handled her in a softer way, but unfortunately for her, I wasn't built that way. With me, Renee was going to get out of that sheltered shit.

"Razor, I..." she stammered, stopping mid-sentence, tears running down her cheeks.

"Don't." My voice came out lower this time, sharp but slower and deliberate. I pulled my right hand off the wheel long enough to snatch the gun up from the floor, click the safety on, and tuck it under my seat. "Don't start that panicked, crying shit now. What's done is done."

Her bottom lip quivered, and she sniffled. "You... you didn't tell me anything before we got here. I just killed that man. Who the fuck was that? Why the fuck you keep dragging me further into this shit?"

"Dragging you into this shit?" I repeated. "Renee, you got in this car on your own free will. You came back to the Airbnb on your own free will. You said you was ridin'. Well, this is what ridin' wit a nigga like me looks like." I tried to spin it so that she was the reason for her being my accomplice.

"No! Don't you dare try to put this on me. You said you needed to make a quick run and if I could ride with you."

"And what you do? Got yo' happy ass in this car at almost one in the morning to ride, right?"

"Yeah, but... not to kill a man, Razor! I have a child! I can't go to prison. I'm **not** going to prison for nobody."

The implication in her tone made me pull the gun from up under the seat and put it to her temple. I was so skilled at this shit, I didn't even need to look her way to know that it was there.

"So, what you saying? You gon' put me in prison, Renee? Cause don't nobody know about this shit except for me, you, and the dead nigga back there. And in case you forgot, a dead man can't tell no tales."

"That's not what I'm saying," she replied, shivering and not from the cold.

"You sure? Cause it sounds a lot like it."

"No, bae. I'm just scared; that's all."

"Oh, aight," I replied, lowering the gun slowly.

Her phone rang for the third time since we'd been out, and I knew it was Santana calling.

"It's Santana again," she confirmed. "I checked the app, and he's not at the hotel anymore."

"At some point, you're gonna have to answer or turn Asia's phone back on, so she can."

"I'll do it in the morning. Right now, I just need to sleep."

We arrived back at the Airbnb, and my phone vibrated as I went to give her instructions. It was my contact calling. "Go inside," I instructed while connecting the call.

"Yeah?"

"Did you get it done?"

I waited for Renee to get out before responding. "Yeah... kinda."

"Fuck you mean kinda? It's either you took care of what I asked you to take care of or you didn't."

"The bitch wasn't there. Caught the brother though."

"And you didn't think to check with me first?!" he snapped.

"Man, look, I saw an opportunity, and I took it. I'm chopping at the body, which will then kill the head."

"And where does that get us if she's not the head? She is the body, which is why I sent you to take her out."

I sighed. This nigga had so many rules and demands but wasn't the boots on the ground. "Aight, man."

"Nah, it's not aight. We out here doing unnecessary ass shit. We got bigger fish to fry at this point. I just got word that Mahogany's father is home. Set up an exchange. Her for the kid. I'll take care of the rest when I touch down."

"When you touch down?"

"Yeah. I'll be there first thing in the morning."

That news had thrown me for a loop and was sure to throw a monkey wrench in my plans. Coolie was home, and he wanted me to give the kid back? Normally, I'd just go along with the plan, so long as it involved me getting paid, but now, this nigga was losing me.

"Aye, man, you killin' me. What's the angle here?"

"The angle is you do what I need you to do, get paid, and be in position for the takeover. See you soon."

The call disconnected, and I sat there, gripping the phone. Slamming my hand against the steering wheel in frustration, I leaned back into the seat to calm myself. It was clear that this nigga had been thinkin' I was just this puppet on a string, but it was time to remind him that I was my own man, and the clock was mine to control. Since he'd decided that a pop up was necessary, I needed to move up the timeframe in which I'd be grabbing that 100K.

Me: Your chance to get your daughter back came sooner than you thought. Meet me at the same spot in the park. Ninety minutes. Bring the bread and come alone. I don't need to tell you what will happen if you don't.

The small ping went off, indicating that the message had been sent. Letting out a tired breath, I stepped out of the car and moved quickly back into the Airbnb. As soon as I opened the door, the soft murmur of voices caught my attention. Thinking it was Renee planning some kind of escape for Beautii, I stood still and listened.

"Ma," Asia's voice came out low and urgent. "I heard it again. There's something... or someone... crying in the back room. I know I'm not buggin."

Renee's voice shot back quickly, reprimanding her. "Asia! I told you to leave it alone."

I remained still, waiting to see how far Renee would let this go. Asia was sharp, a little too sharp for her age. That was a problem. Nosey kids in situations like this caused problems.

"Ma, is somebody back there? You always tellin' me to mind my business, but I heard it. It woke me up outta my sleep. Crying. What's going on?" Her voice was a mixture of fear and curiosity.

"Asia, you didn't hear shit!" Renee whispered back harshly. "I'm not gonna tell you again."

"You said Daddy sent us here to make sure we're safe. How come he hasn't called to check in?"

"I spoke to him while I was out. He checked in."

"Were you able to get me a charger for my phone while you were out?"

"Damn, no. I forgot."

"Wait, Ma. You hear that? The cryi..."

I stepped forward, making my presence known. My Timberland boots against the hardware floor silenced the both of them immediately. Asia froze and scooted over next to her mother on the couch, while Renee put on a brave face.

"Hey, I need y'all to get in the car. I just got a call from Santana. We gotta move." I lightened my tone a little to one of protection rather than cold and calculating. After listening to their conversation, it was clear that some part of Asia didn't trust me or the arrangement.

Asia hesitated, but Renee grabbed her by the wrist and picked her coat up from the couch, gesturing for her to put it on. Moving toward the door, I could see reluctance written all over Asia's face, but she walked in front of her mother. I jerked Renee back by her arm briefly, hissing into her ear.

"Listen to me." My voice was low enough that Asia wouldn't hear. "If she talks — if she even thinks about saying something — you die. You understand me?"

Renee's eyes filled with tears that she blinked back. "I understand."

I squeezed her arm, just to let her feel the gravity of my words. Then, I loosened my grip and nodded toward the door. "I'll be out in a minute."

Shaken but desperate to protect her kid, I watched as she exited behind her, climbed into the backseat, and shut the door. I wasn't worried about her running off. She was operating out of sheer fear. Fear was necessary — it kept people in line. I didn't waste any more time. Heading into the back room, I opened the closet door where Beautii lay, curled up, her back rested against the wall. Her head shot up then fell at the sight of me.

"You're going home," I said flatly.

She blinked at me with a questionable look. Beautii had already figured out how to survive a fucked-up situation, so I expected nothing more than the look she gave. I helped her stand slowly and threw my hoodie over her head. Taking out my phone, I sent a text to Renee.

> Me: Keep Asia occupied. I'm coming out now.

By the time I got Beautii outside, the car was still running, and I hoped Renee was doing her job well enough. Popping the trunk, I picked Beautii up and put her inside. Putting my hand to my mouth, I gave her a knowing glare, letting her know to stay quiet before closing the trunk back. Sliding into the driver's seat, I glanced back at Renee through the rearview mirror and nodded. I then turned the mirror to Asia. Her head was down and in her iPad, exactly where it needed to be — on YouTube and out of grown folks' business.

Turning the music up, I headed for the meeting place, planning to be there before the time given. This would be the last exchange for me, and then I planned to let the chips fall where they may.

Chapter Sixteen

SANTANA

THE CALL TO MY MOTHER DROPPED ONCE I TOLD HER I needed her, so I sent a text instead of dialing back. The text went unanswered minutes too long for me. I needed help and resources, and she was the only one I could trust to get me those things even if she had to go through a third party. She was the only person who didn't side eye me or question my motives — at least not out loud. A few agonizing moments later, my phone lit up.

> Ma: What's going on, Santana? I'm still at the hospital with the family, and we just got hit with more devastating news. We're still tryna piece things together.

I didn't care to know what was going on at the hospital. Right now, what I had going on was more important than anything.

> Me: Renee and Asia aren't at the hotel. They're stuff is here, but I can't find them anywhere.

> Ma: ...you think maybe they just went out to the store?

I thought about my response before I texted because my frustration was going to answer for me, and it wasn't going to be anything nice.

> Me: No, Ma. They didn't go to the store. I've tried calling Renee, and she's not picking up. I think Asia's phone is dead, and her i...

I stopped typing, realizing that I had tried the phones and not Asia's iPad. She always carried it around like it was welded to her hand. She'd also told me that she'd set it up to share its location with me.

"In case of emergencies, Dad. Or if I'm ever punished and Mommy doesn't take it from me because she thinks I only use it for schoolwork." I remembered her clever smile when she told me how she'd work around her punishments.

> Me: I'll figure it out.

Clicking out of our text thread, I didn't bother waiting to see what her response would be. I wasn't about to let her concern for what she was dealing with take precedence over my missing family. So, if I had to ride out alone, that was exactly what I was gonna do. Navigating to the "Find My iPhone" app, I loaded it. The phone took a few seconds to search, and there it was — a blinking green dot on the map. Zooming in on the dot, I clicked it to get a location. Staten Island.

"Staten Island?" I questioned out loud. Renee didn't even know anyone in New York. Why the hell would they be out there?

Starting the car up, I prompted the GPS to direct me to the address. It showed that the iPad's location was stamped there not long ago. As I went to pull off, a text notification popped up. It was from an iCloud email.

> TripleA@icloud.com: Dad, it's me. I'm with Mommy and Uncle. I think something weird is going on. When are you coming to get us?

The time stamp was just a few minutes ago. I hit the FaceTime button to call the number, only for it not to connect. This shit was getting stranger by the second, but the answers were in Staten Island, so I made my way there.

THE STREETS FELT TOO QUIET WHEN I FINALLY PULLED ONTO the block of the address that Asia's iPad was last pinged. It was late, but something about the stillness of the streets felt manufactured, like the peace was hiding something worse beneath it. I parked across the street from a row of townhomes. The green dot on my phone's map flashed ominously, showing me that the iPad was there or had been at some point.

Shutting off the engine, I scanned the area, trying to figure out my next move. I knew whatever I planned to do, I had to move smart and cautiously. I had no back up or lookout. However, my adrenaline and need to make sure my family was safe was all the push I needed. The houses all looked the same under the night sky, and nobody was out walking the street or even poking their head out of a window.

Trust your gut, I told myself.

Stepping out of the car, I picked the nearest townhome and moved toward it. Although my muscles were tense, I moved with purpose and anticipation. Each second stretched longer as I got closer to the door until I lifted my hand to knock — and heard a gun cock behind me. I froze.

"I knew yo' ass was up to no fuckin' good." The voice was feminine but sharp. "You better say something that make sense, or I'ma put a hole in the back of yo' big ass head. Talk, Santana!" She shoved the gun into my head, not caring if it went off.

Slowly, I turned, my rage mirroring hers. She was shorter than me, wiry, but with more fire in her than plenty of niggas I'd gone toe to toe with in my lifetime. She had the gun trained on me, eyes remaining steady.

"Morae," I said slowly, keeping my voice even. "I don't know what the fuck is goin on, but I'm here on some personal shit. An emergency."

"Yeah, well, me too. Somebody killed my brother tonight, and the car the son of a bitch sped off in led me here. I knew we should've never trusted yo' ass from the moment you stepped foot in the club." Her finger rested on the trigger comfortably, and I knew that if I didn't say something that made sense to her, there was a likely chance that I'd be killed.

"I don't have shit to do with your brother being dead." I held my hand up and gestured to my phone. "My daughter. Her iPad led me here. Renee and my daughter are missing."

She narrowed her eyes at me, testing the truth in my response. "What makes you think she'd be here out of all places?"

"I already told you — her iPad pinged this location through the "Find My iPhone" app. I don't know nothing about your brother being killed. The answers to both of our questions may very well be behind this door, but we won't know unless we go in. So, you gotta put the gun down, Ma."

Her lip curled slightly, but she didn't lower the gun. "I ain't puttin' shit down. Like I said, I don't trust you. Move out the way." I stepped to the side, and she lifted her foot, sending a swift kick to the door. The lock snapped easily, and the two of us stepped inside the dark, stagnant air of the townhome.

"You take the front, and I'll take the back," I suggested, closing the front door.

"Santana, I swear if you try any funny shit..."

"Didn't you hear me say my kid is missing now? I ain't tryna do shit but find her and Renee." I walked toward the back, leaving her standing there.

The place was roomy, and as I navigated each room, checking for any signs of someone having been there, it was clear that there was activity at some point. In one of the rooms, the bed was unmade, sheets sprawled about the bed as if someone had laid there or fucked. I did a thorough check, and after finding nothing more there, I went to the next room. Coming up empty, I hit the last bedroom in the back. As I searched, it became apparent that someone had been in this room as well. I heard the door creak and knew it was Morae behind me.

"Did you check the closet?"

"I was about to."

Not waiting on me, she pulled the closet closest to the door open. "Shit."

"What?" I asked, rushing to her side just as she bent down to pick it up.

"Beautii," she said with her hand covering her mouth.

"Beautii what? This hers?"

She held up the bracelet for me to see. It looked expensive, and upon further inspection, I concluded that it belonged to someone with a small wrist. "It's the Cartier bracelet Mahogany brought her last year for her birthday. Look, it's engraved."

The engraving read: *To That Girl, Beautii.*

"She was here." Taking out her phone, Morae typed away while I tried to piece things together in my head.

If Beautii was here and my daughter's iPad was here, where the fuck was everybody, and who had them? As I racked my brain, my phone vibrated. It was a FaceTime call from Asia's phone.

I connected the call quickly, and all I could see was darkness in her background. **"Asia, baby. Where are you? Hello, can you hear me?"**

"Dad, I can hear you," she whispered. **"I'm scared. Can you come and get me?"**

"Yes, baby. I can come and get you right now. You just gotta tell me where you are and what you see." Leaving the room with Mo on my heels, I headed for the front door.

"I... I... I don't know. It's dark out here. Mommy told me not to call, but I'm nervous, and she and Uncle are actin' weird. Dad, I... I think I saw Be..." The call disconnected before she could get the last word out.

"See if the iPad pings where she is now. You gotta hurry up before we miss it." Mo pushed.

Clicking on the contact, I located the map, and there was the blinking green dot again but on a different location. Leaning over me, Morae touched the screen and zoomed in. Quickly mapping it, we got a location that was about an hour from here.

"Who's the uncle?" She pried. "I thought you didn't have no people here other than those you came to reunite with?"

Sensing some kind of betrayal in the air that had my daughter feeling like danger was imminent, I answered truthfully. "Razor. He's my best friend, and Asia calls him Uncle. He came here from Cali with me."

"I can't say that I'm surprised. Now you know while you plottin' on someone else's demise, there could be someone in your own backyard plottin' to take you up outta here. And your plan may not have been to kill either one of us, but you were up to something. And that something ultimately cost us the people we love. I'ma say this. When you see that nigga, you betta squeeze until the clip is empty, or I'ma only shoot once." She gave me dead eyes before walking back to her car.

Reality hit me, and I surmised that Razor was playin' me right in my face. And from what Asia mentioned about her mother, she had in some way included herself in the game — just not on my side. I straightened up as the pieces in my mind snapped into place and jogged over to my car. I had to kill my childhood tonight but not without an explanation first.

Chapter Seventeen

MAHOGANY

As I sat with Tiff, my phone vibrated with a text from the kidnapper. He wanted to push up the meeting time and of course wanted me to come alone. Figuring something must've gone wrong on his end and his desperation was mounting, I decided I would use it to my advantage, and this time, I wasn't going alone. Fuck that. This was my city, and I was no longer letting some bloodsucker decide how shit would operate. After texting Justice to meet me out front, I also sent a text to Briscoe to meet me at home. I hadn't heard from him, and I didn't want to keep him out of the loop, but I had no intentions on waiting around for his response. Rubbing Tiff's hand, she awoke and squeezed mine back. .

"Go head and say it," she let out. "I should've told y'all what was going on sooner, so y'all could've went on without me."

"Nope. I'll let you deal with you for that. Oh, and Money too. And ya mom and dad. I know you were faking sleep when they came in."

Her eyes widened. "Y'all told Money? When he get back? Oh, my God, y'all can't hold water."

"He's been here. He left with Mo. Should be headed back this way now."

She sucked her teeth. "Now he gon' come in here with his bullshit after the doctor said I'm okay. I just overexerted myself."

"And went into cardiac arrest, Tiffany. This shit is no small thing. You gotta sit down for a while, boo. There's been enough death going around in our family. I can't lose you too."

She hung her head. "You're not gonna lose me. I promise. And we're not gonna lose anyone else. Any update on Beautii?"

"Yeah. Before everything happened with you, I was coming downstairs to let y'all know that the guy called and said I had another chance to get her."

"And this time, you will. Have a shootout with that nigga if that's what it takes. Dudas came by Mo's house when we were over there. He suggested that we get the police involved. Mo cancelled that idea quick. You know it would've made him feel good just to know we went about things the 'right' way for once."

"Dudas is dead, Tiffany." I was trying to find the right time or even the right way to tell her, but there was none.

"What?" she cried. "When? Who? Where's Mo? Damn."

"They brought him here tonight. Someone shot him three times in the chest. Mo and Money already know. They went over to their dad's house to tell him."

"Damn," she let out again. I reached over and hugged her tight. The door to her room opened, and we both looked up to see Money walking in.

"Come here, bae," Tiff said with her arms stretched out. Money walked over and practically fell into her arms. The emotions poured out of him as she rocked him back-and-forth like a baby.

I wished that I could console them both in the moment, but once again, I was trying to beat the time.

"I gotta go, y'all. The ransom exchange was moved up."

Money looked up and went to speak, but I stopped him. "I know, bro. I know. You're right where I need you to be. I'm gonna be fine."

"Bring our baby back, Hogany."

"I will."

Leaving the room, I ran into my father and Dough, who were standing just outside, talking.

"I'm going to get Beautii," I informed the both of them. "I'm taking Justice with me."

"Okay," my father said without a rebuttal.

"Okay?"

"Yes. While you handle that, we going to the source to put an end to all this shit."

"The source?"

"Yeah. Mommy and Tionne will stay here with Tiffany."

"Money will look after them," Dough added.

"Let me know when you have Beautii." My father pulled me in for a hug and whispered in my ear. "Show these motherfuckas why I put you in charge."

With that, I walked out of the hospital, meeting Justice at the entrance.

"You ready?" he asked.

I tossed him my car keys. "You drive. We're going to get my baby. First, we gotta pick up the money from my house."

On the way to my house, I prayed. I not only prayed for myself, but I prayed for my family. Once this was all over, I knew we'd all need a vacation. Not for fun or relaxation but for a peace of mind. I didn't know how long it would take to get that sense of normalcy back, but as long as we worked at it together, I knew we would. The ringing of my phone caught my attention. I glanced at the screen and saw Santana's name lit up. My jaw tightened as I swiped to answer it.

"Santana," I said, my voice dripping with irritation. After having to yoke his bitch up earlier, I didn't have many words for him.

"I'm heading to Manhattan," he said with urgency.

"Are you telling me this because you have a lead on where Beautii is?"

"I think so," he answered, exhaling heavily. **"Asia and Renee are missing. I tracked Asia's iPad to an address in Staten Island.**

When I got there, Mo was there. Apparently, the same address or person connected to the address has something to do with her brother being killed.”

Something protective and primal stirred in my chest. **“Santana, you’re saying a lot but not saying what I need to know, which is what does any of this have to do with Beautii?”**

He paused, and his hesitation alone made my heartbeat race.

“Mahogany,” he said slowly, **“while we were at the house, we found a bracelet. A bracelet Mo recognized from Beautii’s birthday last year. I know who has Beautii.”**

The car felt like it was shrinking, and beads of sweat cluttered on my forehead while I gripped the door handle.

“Who has my kid, Santana?”

“Razor. My best friend, Razor, has Beautii, Asia, and Renee.”

“Excuse me?” I said carefully, my voice deadly. **“You mean to tell me that the motherfucka that done snatched my daughter out of my mama house is your fuckin’ best friend?! A motherfucka I don’t know from Adam?!”** I roared.

“I don’t know how or why,” he continued, his words tumbling out. **“I just know I’m heading to Manhattan where I tracked Asia’s iPad.”**

Forcing myself to slow my breath, I spoke. **“Send me the location.”**

I heard him pause on the other end then a soft ding on my phone as the notification came through. Opening it, my pulse jumped again as I realized the address matched the one I’d been given.

“Make this shit make sense to me, Santana. What does your people gain from taking Beautii? Because this shit is far from a random play. You do something foul in Cali, and that nigga followed you here? Or you been in cahoots the whole time?”

Santana sighed heavily. **“I don’t know, Mahogany. Razor’s been my boy since we were kids. Yeah, he’s known to do some wild shit but nothing like this. He loyal. This shit ain’t adding up.”**

“And that means what to me?” I snapped. **“That nigga got my baby, yo baby, and yo bitch. Fuck is you sayin’ to me about**

loyalty? There's no 'this ain't adding up.' The only thing that adds up is the fact that I'm getting my child back tonight and sending yo childhood friend to the afterlife."

"Mahogany, I'm on my way now. We gon'..."

I hung up in his face. There wasn't shit else I needed to hear from Santana. He'd said enough.

"What's the word?" Justice asked.

"You want the short version or the long one?"

"Sum it up for me. We can talk more in detail after we handle business."

"Some nigga named Razor has Beautii. Santana's so-called best friend. He has her and Santana's family."

"Aight. We got a name, and Santana obviously knows his face. That works in our favor. I'm sure he don't know Santana pullin' up too."

"This shit just keeps getting more and more insane."

"It's gonna be over real soon. This time, we're going in with the upper hand."

"What you mean?"

"I was gonna fill you in, but before I could, we were at the hospital with ya girl. I reached out to my people and sent them back to the park to do another sweep of it. I had them map out the whole area. So, now, we know of the different exits, entryways, and cuts."

I turned my head to look at him fully and nodded. "I appreciate that. Send me the tab for their services once we get settled."

"That won't be necessary. I told you I'm here to help."

As we turned to pull onto my street, I made him come to a full stop. "Turn the car around. I'm not giving this nigga another fuckin' dime. We're not negotiating either. We're going straight to the meet up spot."

Without questioning my plan, Justice bust a U-turn, and we were on our way to the exchange spot. Only I wouldn't be exchanging money for Beautii. I was taking a nigga's life.

THE PARK LOOMED AHEAD, QUIET AND DARK. I DIDN'T FEEL fear, only sharp focus. Justice parked the car, and I told him to get out and get in the backseat. Stepping out, I scanned the street. My phone buzzed with a text from Santana, letting me know he was close. As I went to put it away, it buzzed again, this time with a message from Morae.

> Mo: I'm in the park. I can see you. I'm behind the bathrooms.

She'd concealed herself well because I couldn't see shit past the street unless I crossed and walked on that side. I texted her back to stay sharp and keep her eyes open. We had another three minutes before we were at the time given to meet. I hoped Santana knew well enough to keep his headlights off when he pulled up. I wanted him right at my side when his best friend arrived. I just knew that putting them face to face would stir up some shit.

Down to the minute mark, Santana still hadn't arrived, so I proceeded to dial who I'd now come to know as Razor's number. The call rang once before he picked up.

"I take it you're here, Ms. Boss Bitch."

"I am."

"Cool. Walk into the park and over to the swings please. It's straight ahead. You can stay on the phone."

I continued ahead. **"Where's Beautii?"**

"She's close by. Keep walking."

I kept moving, keeping my eyes straight ahead so as to not alert him of anyone else's presence. Making it to the swing sets, I could see him swinging without a care in the world. Ending the call, I slowed down my stride.

"Wassup, Ms. Boss Bitch? It's good to see you in person." The man before me was dark as night with a clean-shaven head that was partially covered by a hoodie. "Emptyhanded, huh? What, you didn't trust me to bring your little girl after the last time?"

"Where is she?"

"You know, all of this didn't start this way. We just wanted something that you weren't willing to just give."

"I don't know what you're talking about, and quite frankly, I don't give a fuck. If this shit is just about money, I can have a half a mill wired to an account of your choice within the hour. I don't give a fuck about money. I just want my kid, and we can all walk away from this shit." I figured reasoning would be the best way for me to get closer to him.

"I mean, it's definitely about the bread. It's also a test of loyalty and family. You know, shit like that. I'm tryna see who our brother is most loyal to."

"Our brother?" I questioned with a raised brow.

"Yeah. Santana. He's not my blood brother, but blood couldn't have made us any closer. But yeah. He's here, right? I mean, according to this app, he's in the park right now."

Just then, Santana appeared from the darkness with his gun raised. "Where the fuck is Renee and Asia?"

"You mean that Renee?" Razor questioned, swinging casually.

I heard a gun cock and felt steel pressed against the back of my head.

"Renee, what the fuck are you doing?!" Santana barked with his gun still trained on Razor, who seemed to be getting a kick out of the show.

"Where's your loyalty, Santana?" Razor taunted. "Is it to the woman you've laid with over ten plus years and made plans with? Or is it to the sister whose throne you've been plotting to take since you touched down? Inquiring minds would like to know."

Nothing that Razor had to say surprised me or made me feel a way. I knew Santana showing up out of the blue wasn't without reason. There was a method to my madness when I decided to bring him into the fold anyway. Santana's eyes shot over to me, and I shrugged.

"How long you been fucking this nigga, Renee?"

"Dawg, she's not gonna answer that. She'd rather you take her ass out right now than to admit that I've been punishing that pussy since you were down on this last bid."

I didn't know how the situation looked to Santana, but it seemed as though Razor was saying anything to get a rise out of us. He must've known he was dying tonight. I'd had enough of the soap opera bullshit though.

Raising my foot, I kicked back hard on Renee's knee, making her cry out and hit the ground. Razor jumped up to run, but I was quicker, pulling my gun from my waist and hitting him twice in the back. I went to turn my attention to Renee, who'd lost control of her gun like an amateur, and saw Morae walking up in Santana's direction with her gun drawn.

"You remember what I said, right, Santana?" She spoke directly to him.

With no words, he stood over Razor and emptied the clip, while Renee watched in horror.

"Where's my daughter?" I asked with my gun trained on her.

"In the trunk of the Lexus LS. It's parked at the end of the block. Asia is in the backseat. Santana, baby, I'm so sor..."

POP! POP!

I sent two shots to her chest. No way I was letting that bitch walk or crawl out of this park alive. She was a fucking accomplice. There was no telling how involved she really was.

"Santana," I called out, still standing over his dead baby mama. "We straight? Or do I have to leave you in this park too?"

"We good."

I nodded and walked back toward the exit to look for the Lexus. When I got to the sidewalk, Justice was already out of the car with his gun at his side.

"The kids are in a Lexus LS," I said to him. "You check the cars on that side; I'll check this side."

I got a few cars down, locating the Lexus immediately. It was dark inside, but I could see a body lying flat in the backseat. I went to pull on the passenger door, and it was locked. I knocked, and the figure didn't move.

"Asia," I called Santana's daughter's name. She popped up, and my heart raced. "It's Mahogany, honey. Open the door."

She did and jumped out, hugging me around my neck. "Please tell me my dad is with you."

"He is, honey. Where's Beautii?"

She turned to the trunk, and I got her drift. "Down here!" Hitting the locks for the front doors, I ran over to the front seat to find the lever for the trunk. Fidgeting around, I heard Justice's voice behind me.

"Let me get it, Ma." I stepped back, and he found the lever in seconds, pulling it to pop the trunk.

"Beautii," I gasped, seeing my baby bound and gagged. "Oh, my God! Beautii, baby, I'm here." Justice came around and helped me pick her up out of the trunk. I took the scarf off her mouth and hugged my baby tight while she cried hard. "Mommy got you. I got you, Beautii."

Chapter Eighteen

COOLIE

THE THING ABOUT SOMEONE WHO WANTS SOMETHING THAT don't belong to them was that they became so fixated on that thing that they couldn't see anything else. They plotted and schemed and often missed the little details in their planning. That was Santana Sr. It took me a minute to piece it all together, but I figured it out eventually; he was the puppet master. And while he thought that he was the only one who had eyes on the board, he clearly forgot who the fuck I was and how far my reach could go.

His downfall wasn't a mystery. It wasn't carefully constructed through conspiracy. It was real simple in fact: his cockiness. Santana's problem was that he didn't have a well thought out plan that he didn't have to seek counsel for. His counselor just happened to be someone I'd known for years. And while I hadn't checked in in a while, I figured it was time to.

"Kiena, has the man been making moves?" I talked into the phone, sitting in the passenger seat of my car while Dough stood watch outside.

"A busy body he has been. He paid for a week of my time, and I've been at his side ever since. Sounds like he sent his son up your way to get reacquainted. But he doesn't believe his junior has what it takes to lead. So, he sent his boy, Razor, up there as backup. It's easier that way, ya

know? The two are best friends, so he won't know what Razor is up to as he gets the orders from Senior. However, it seems Razor has gone rogue."

"So, Senior wants a seat, huh?"

She laughed lightly. "Come on, love. Who would want just a seat at such a prestigious organization, Coolie? He wants The Table itself."

"Thanks, Kiena. Check your account in an hour."

"He's planning a flight out in the morning to your neck of the woods. You'll have the flight itinerary shortly."

"Always thorough."

"It's how you've always taught me to be. Chow."

Santana thought **he** was untouchable. He thought wrong.

The thing about figuring out who was behind the drama was it made the rest of the problem real simple. You just had to move before they realized they'd been exposed. Santana had slipped. Granted, he'd been able to get his shit off beforehand. Paris's death. Dudas's death. And Beautii's kidnapping, but that was as far as he'd get. At some point during the wee hours of the morning, Mahogany had called and let us know she found Beautii, and she was getting her settled at home. That was good. I made it a point to go see my grandbaby as soon as I tied up this loose end. Santana was still in play, and he wouldn't land on New York soil unless it was on my terms.

The next day, I was up early after getting two hours of sleep. I slipped out of bed, careful not to wake Nette, and got myself together. I texted Dough and Justice to make sure they were set, and they confirmed their positions. I'd tracked Santana's flight, mapped out the arrival time, and secured a rental car that could pass for an Uber.

"Where you going this early?" Nette asked as I walked out of the bathroom fully dressed.

"Tying up loose ends." Going over to her side of the bed, I kissed her lips. "No questions," I said before she could fix her lips to ask any. "Just know I'll be back."

"Okay. I love you."

"I love you more, Nette."

Grabbing a coat from the closet and my FN, I headed out the door.

The airport was easy for people to disappear in the hustle and bustle of things, especially one as busy as Laguardia. However, Santana's face was burned into my memory, so I knew I wouldn't miss him. Parking in the designated pickup spot, I slapped an Uber sticker on the dash and waited. The second I saw him exit the terminal with his carry-on slung over his shoulder, I pulled up right in front of him. I'd had Kiena "book" an Uber for him, so he wouldn't be suspicious.

Rolling down the window just as he scanned the lineup of cars, I called out to him. "Santana?"

"Yeah," he replied.

"I'm your ride," I said, casually motioning to the passenger seat.

While it had been years since we'd seen each other, nothing had changed about me except the fact that I had a few grays in my hair that I rocked proudly, and I'd bulked up. Today, I rocked a mustache and had a fitted cap and sunglasses on to hide my eyes. Santana slid in the backseat of the Honda CRV with no questions. That was the problem with people like him — too sure of themselves to clock a set up when it was staring them right in the face.

The ride was a quiet one with him busying himself on the phone and me consciously making detours with him not questioning one turn.

"You from here?" I asked.

"Nah, just visiting on family business. We taking a short cut or something? According to my app, you should've taken a right back there, my man."

"Warehouse district," I said simply. "There's a detour on the main roads."

I watched him shrug his shoulders in the rearview mirror, accepting my excuse. Big mistake.

Pulling up to the warehouse, it loomed ahead — rundown and forgotten by everyone except for those who did business in places like this. People like me. I parked on the side entrance, and by the time he'd realized something was off, I was already out of the car, opening his door with my gun drawn.

"Get the fuck outta the car."

"What the hell is this?"

I pulled off the glasses, hat, and mustache. "It's my welcome home celebration. You're the special guest. Get out and walk."

Inside the dimly lit warehouse, Dough stepped out of the shadows. He locked eyes with Santana and shook his head. "I knew we'd meet again and on these terms."

"Have a seat," I said, pointing to the only chair in the middle of the floor.

"I ain't…" *POP!* I hit him in the leg. "Ahhh, shit!"

"Not in the mood for the tough guy shit today, Santana. Sit the fuck down."

When he took a seat, Dough went to tie him to it.

"You schemed. You plotted. Pulling strings like you thought nobody was watching. And for what? Huh? All cause you want a nigga legacy? That's why you came for my family?"

He didn't respond, just gave me a smug look. "It's cool, my nigga. You ain't gotta talk. I ain't come here expecting you to admit to anything. I want you to see what you couldn't break though."

The sounds of heels clicking on the concrete could be heard as Mahogany walked inside with a gas can in hand. Dressed in an all-black suit, she was donned in jewelry, looking nothing like what she'd been through in the past twenty-four hours. My daughter looked like every bit of the boss I'd groomed her to be.

"Good morning, Mr. Santana," she spoke while dousing him in gasoline. "We never had the pleasure of meeting. It's fucked up that it has to be under these circumstances, but sometimes you gotta play the cards you're dealt. You've caused me so much grief and agony in the last twenty-four hours, it's only right I return that feeling back to you. Only this will burn a lot longer." Pulling a match from her slacks, she flicked it and threw it in his lap.

"No, wait! Oh, shit!" He hopped around in the chair as best he could, but nothing could stop the flames that engulfed his body.

"Thanks, Dad," she said, kissing my cheek. "I gotta get back home to Beautii."

"No problem, baby."

"Calculating and effective," Dough said, sliding his hands in his pockets. "What about Junior? How you think he gon' feel about this?"

"How it's supposed to be. Clean up here. I don't want him traced back to us. And as far as Santana, he can feel dead if he wants smoke behind this. In the meantime, I have Justice watching his every move in Cali."

Dough nodded, already pulling out his phone to make the necessary calls.

The Table was our legacy. Wouldn't nobody come up against it and live to tell the story. And trust, when shit went left, we would make it Wright.

Epilogue

ONE YEAR LATER

THE SUNLIGHT FILTERED THROUGH THE TREES, GIVING WAY for a perfect day for us all to come together. It was warm today — a bright day to celebrate two beautiful souls that were taken from us just a year ago. We all decided to come out to the park for a balloon releasing for Dudas and Paris. Even with the weight of everything still hanging somewhere deep in our hearts, we all felt that this would be the best way to remember them.

I thought back to how much had changed over the course of a year. I glanced over at Beautii, who stood with my parents and Justice, and thought about all that my now thirteen-year-old had been through. Over the next few months after finding her, Briscoe and I enrolled her in counseling. It was the best decision we could've made for our child so as to not allow her to sink into depression. I didn't want that for my baby. And not only had her counseling helped her tremendously, it also helped our coparenting relationship.

Beautii being kidnapped made me quickly realize that I had to do a better job at juggling everything I had going on. My family constantly reminded me that it wasn't my fault, but in the back of my mind, I saw different. Over time, I'd buried that guilt for the sake of not smothering

Beautii to make up for it. It also helped that Justice wasn't afraid to get on my head when those thoughts surfaced. He was a good man. My good man now.

As we trekked up the hill so that we were high enough to let the balloons go, I could hear Tiffany fussing from behind me.

"No, seriously, Montez, I don't need help walking ten feet."

"You're eight months pregnant. Almost nine. You lucky I ain't carrying you up this hill," Money argued. "Just hold the balloons and stop being so stubborn."

Ever since that cardiac scare that put her in the hospital, Money was on her ass like white on rice. And when they found out she was pregnant, it was over. He wasn't fuckin' around.

"You aggravating, you know that?" she countered. I looked back to see him slap her on the butt, and she giggled.

"Alright now. Cut all that out in front of my son," Morae let out, holding DJ in her arms.

"Here she go," I egged on. "You know she don't play about her son."

"And don't." She laughed.

After Paris' death, her great aunt was diagnosed with cancer. And with Ms. Reece becoming his legal guardian, she had papers drawn up to say that she wanted Morae to take DJ in the event of her passing. Of course, his father wouldn't have it and fought Mo tooth and nail in court, but by the grace of God, Paris' last will and testament had specifically noted that she didn't want his father to have custody and provided evidence as to why, and the judge all but placed DJ right in Mo's care on the last day of court. None of us knew just how much Paris suffered at the hands of her bd before getting with Mo. It was all a blessing in disguise.

We hadn't heard anything from Santana after that night at the park, and I didn't know if my mother had kept in contact, but I preferred it this way. The way I saw it, this was all the family I'd ever need.

"Y'all ready?" Mo's dad asked.

We all lifted our balloons and nodded.

"To Paris and Dudas. May your life in the afterlife be as blessed as it was here on Earth." We let the white and blue balloons go in the air, and I felt a peace come over my body. A silent job well done.

I wouldn't trade this life for anything or anyone. This was The Table run by the baddest, most thorough bitches you'd ever seen.

THE END

Also By Nai

Wrapped Up In A Hitta's Love For Christmas

Yours For The Taking

Seizing A Gangsta's Heart For The Summer

Thug Me The Right Way

Thug Me The Right Way 2

Thug Me The Right Way 3

A Summer To Remember With My Hitta

Snatched Up By A Hitta

Wet Dreams On Lockdown: The Unit Manager

Santa Sent Me A Real One For Christmas

Bossin' Up On The Plug

Bossin' Up On The Plug 2

In The Trenches With My Hitta

n The Trenches With My Hitta 2

Stealing A Queenpin's Heart

Stealing A Queenpin's Heart 2

A Piece of A Hustler's Heart

A Piece of A Hustler's Heart 2

A Thug's Love Mended My Heart

A Thug's Love Mended My Heart 2

A Summer To Remember With My New York Bae

A Summer Fling In New York

His Hood Love Gave Me Life

His Hood Love Gave Me Life 2

My Thug, My Sanctuary

Thug Kisses For Christmas

For The Love Of My Savage

Charge It To The Game

Charge It To The Game 2

Charge It To The Game 2
A Summer To Remember With My Hitta
Snatched Up By A Hitta
Santa Sent Me A Real One For Christmas
Wet Dreams On Lockdown: The Unit Manager
Thug Me The Right Way 2
Thug Me The Right Way 3
Seizing A Gangsta's Heart For The Summer
Yours For The Taking
Wrapped Up In A Hitta's Love For Christmas
By **Nai**

A Set Up For Revenge
A Set Up For Revenge 2
Wet Dreams On Lockdown: The Librarian
By **Ashley Williams**

Trickin' On A Heaux For Christmas
Homie Hoppin' For The Holidays
Wet Dreams On Lockdown: The Female C.O
Letters Of His Love
By **Telia Teanna**

The State's Witness
The State's Witness 2
The State's Witness 3
This Time Won't You Save Me
This Time Won't You Save Me 2
His Summer Side Piece
A Holiday Heist
By **Kyiris Ashley**

Stuck In The Trenches
Stuck In The Trenches 2
By **Huff Tha Great**

Melted The Heart Of A Menace
Wet Dreams On Lockdown: Lieutenant Grace
By **P. Wise**

Merry Trapmas
By **Mia Sky**

Thug Me The Right Way
By **DiamondATL & Nai**

Wet Dreams On Lockdown: The Counselor
By **Paris Iman**

Wet Dreams On Lockdown: The Male C.O
By **Tamyra Griffin**

Wet Dreams On Lockdown: The Captain
By **TN Jones**

Wet Dreams On Lockdown: The Warden
By **Shawnice**

Atlantastan
Atlantastan 2
By **Chris Green**

IN The Streetz
IN The Streetz 2
IN The Streetz 3
IN The Streetz 4

By **Tron Hill**

Hittin' Licks For The Holidays: New York
By **Freshh Moneyy**

Coming Soon From
URBAN AINT DEAD

The Hottest Summer Ever 2
THE G-CODE
Tales 4rm Da Dale 2
How To Invest In The Stock Market From Prison
By **Elijah R. Freeman**

Good Girls Gone Rogue 3
By **Manny Black**

Despite The Odds 2
By **Juhnell Morgan**

Foreva Your Gangsta
By **Nai**

This Time Won't You Save Me 3
Healing The Heart Of A Detroit Gangsta
By **Kyiris Ashley**

Atlantastan 3
By **Chris Green**

IN The Streetz 5
By **Tron Hill**